INCISION PRESS

Take It Outside

An anthology of Queer and Trans Desire

Contents

Foreword

Foreword from Orlando Silver

I am sitting in bed as I write this. My white sheets are tangled because I never make my bed, and the bed is pushed up hard against the wall because I never bring anyone home. My home is for writing. For 3am scrawled, long narratives. My home is for the 6am moments where before I can even register what I am doing, I reach next to my bed, grab my laptop and start typing.

Outside my window, the Australian Summer sun is relentless. There is body impact from the heat. I am thinking, I should take a break today. I should read more. I should walk, listen to the great hum of cicadas like a holy mantra, I should make space for the rest that my body needs.

But that's not who I am right now. Right now is the time to work. That's why this book exists, and why the next one will come after it.

Many years ago during one of the most epic breakups of my life I went to a Buddhist conference in Sydney. I was a very devout Buddhist at the time. It was slowly saving my life. Incredibly, the fierce warrior that is Ani Tenzin Palmo was there. This is a woman who had spent 12 years in the remote Himalayas living and meditating in a cave. She was everything I dreamed of being: she gave zero fucks about anything; but at the same time was the heart of compassion.

A young woman who didn't know any better bumped into Ani Tenzo in the foyer of the conference. I saw it. Ani was surrounded by her attendants who would likely spend most of their remaining lives in service to this great woman. I myself was too scared to even look her in the eye.

"Oh!" She said, "I wanted to ask you. I just don't seem to have any time for meditation. I set alarms, I have an altar, I do all the things, but I just don't seem to get there. What do I do?"

Ani Tenzon Palmo placed a gentle hand on her shoulder. She looked directly at her, smiled and said, "Remember that you might die tomorrow. You could die after lunch. We don't know." Then she laughed and said, "That should keep you pretty focused."

For those of us who arrive on the page with power, particularly in the political climate we are in, there is nothing more critical than this concept. There is no time to lose.

Writing uncensored queer pleasure and intimacy is political work. This is my body. This is the language I use. This is how I want to be touched. This is what loss feels like. This is what it takes to stay alive. This is what I need, from you, right now.

I am indebted to the writers in these pages. The intensity and nuance of NoN BiNarY BiRo, who remains a hero to me over these many years. The soft, persuasive heat of the marvellous erin riley. The deft, loving embrace of Jaymie Wagner. I feel the privilege of hosting the always incredibly sexy Anna Sansom. Buy everything that Anna writes if you can.

I hold in highest regard the fierce Mx Nillin Lore, for both the expertise in writing and the ongoing community leadership. The same for Christian Pan, whose work ethic matches my own (there is no higher praise). What joy to have the depth of skill that Des De DeVivo offers us - a diamond in the rough.

If you don't know Leo Wilder, then welcome home to true smut. Leo is the best one-handed read for anyone that needs a butch in their life. Lilith Young always brings me something that feels like a sucker punch. Clear, direct and good.

My body was thrilled with adrenaline within the first five lines of the piece by SoftBoss. Likewise the sexy shower scene by Ryder West. You can't say I didn't warn you. Try not to get lube on the pages. Come to mention it, this also applies to the piece by Sharon Penance!! Goddamn. Too good.

I was shocked and moved by Cosimo Vazquez - watching the expansive growth of his voice has been a privilege. He pushes harder every time. I see you, Cosimo. The dear, loving fuckery that Cash Torn offers us in these pages simply delights me, as does the hotness that is Tiger Salmon.

The exploration of intimacy and desire within Jordan Asher's story makes me swoon. I adore the unflinching cutting strength of the piece by The IE; and Macsen K. Rhaff has brought us something darker and wilder than I knew I needed. I can't wait to see what Macsen writes next.

I saw early drafts of the work by Mx Slate Ruins so I knew it would be this good. Their piece holds the exact spirit of revolution and pleasure that stops my heart. On the other hand, I had never heard of Ma Bo, and now I need to read everything this writer creates. Give me more please.

My last acknowledgment here is for my friend Cash Torn. Thank you for the anchoring. You are so important to me, and I have valued your skill more that I have words to say. Long may our editorial partnership, and our friendship, flourish.

See you all on the page.
  Orlando

Foreword from Cash Torn

I was introduced to Orlando Silver in a beautifully serendipitous way. A lover bought me Soft Fruit, one of his earlier publications, as a sweet gift for no other reason than they thought I would enjoy it.

I began following Orlando on Instagram and Substack, then on a whim, signed up for his ridiculously affordable Write Hard classes, despite having barely written for many years. Those Write Hard classes were a shining light during an otherwise dark time as I grappled with the onset of disability in a Western capitalist society. But I kept showing up, and I kept writing.

Then some interesting life events threw Orlando and I into the same place at the same time in the 'real world' and a wonderful friendship grew from our common struggle of being gluten free *and* vegan, the trials and tribulations of being a Daddy, and of course, writing.

This anthology encompasses so many things for me. This book is the fruit of the labours of lust and love and collaboration in a celebration of queer joy, vulnerability and sexuality. We need queer art as a means of connection, to hear our stories in our own voices, to see our own bodies truthfully depicted, to reflect our desires, and most importantly in my opinion, as documented proof that we are desired *and* desirable.

Thank you Orlando, for bringing me into Incision Press, and for patiently extending deadlines every time my health got in my way. Thank you to every writer who worked through edits with me, who gracefully took my advice on board and also challenged me on my suggestions, you are all incredible.

And thank you to my boy, the sexiest and most patient man in the world, for always listening to my hyperfixations, for loving me as I am, and for always being down to join in eating broccoli with chick'n nuggets for dinner.

To all my past and future iterations; stay weird, be kind to yourself because often life will not be, and for fuck sake keep writing.

Cash

1

25 by NoN BiNarY BiRo

It's summer. London. Hot still. Mottled light. Parakeets fizz like green lollipops in the sky. August folds in on itself. Ice creams and tepid beers, mini skirts and sticky T-shirts. Buses belch up gas.The underground is soup-stuffy. Pavements sizzle. My friend has moved into the apartment but my friend is away. In France, with their mum. We leave voice notes for each other. I talk about dating, my friend talks about their mum. I receive little missives about hotels, meals out, the ferry ride to Dieppe.

We're still learning how to live together and how to live apart, despite knowing each

other for over 20 years. I tell them that I want to date a femme.

Need one, I say.

Right.

High. Kinky. Queer. Dialled up.

Dialled up?

Owning it.

Wow.

Exactly.

***

A week later, I meet you. Sunday Bank Holiday. In a cocktail bar in Dalston.

We drink in the late afternoon. You talk of Tennessee, of Dublin, of theology, of raving, of maths' club, of sex. Your smile shatters me. Your laugh is swift. Your limbs shimmer.

You look bright, amazing, maybe a little broken. A softness like sand sifting through you. You talk of decades of pain, disability, worry, family stuff.

I'm tired. Hungover (I worked the night before). I'm wearing a jacket and jeans. My skin is sun-kissed, ash-stained. I listen to the medley of your voice. Try to locate your wandering accent. You rabbit on, tell tales, crack funnies. You are effortlessly amusing. I wonder if this is an attempt to mask your sorrow, but later learn, it's your pathway to being accepted.

I scratch my hair and lean in. Spin out as you speak. My mind unravels. I wonder if you'll grip onto the sheets, cry out, buckle as I fuck you. I wonder if you'll grab at my arse, rip my skin, break into me. I wonder if you'll let me hit you. And where. Which part of your body. How hard and how long. I wonder how many partners you will need. How much attention. How much praise (I have a hunch this is your kink and later learn that it is). I wonder if I can choke you, grab you by the throat, knock your neck sideways like a screw. I wonder if I can attach you to the bedroom door handle with my dog lead, blindfold you, tie you up with belts. I wonder if you'll agree to draw up a contract. Just so we can write it down, everything, list our proclivities. Every little detail.

You catch my hand. Bring my focus back to the bar. You offer me your glass. I sip your drink - Twinkle, French 75, Penicillin - I don't remember what I order.

I have to start with a question, it's my priority, I need to follow through. You catch your breath. Your teeth click. Spittle forms at the edge of your mouth. I could drink it.

Do you define as femme? I say.

I need an answer. I feel restless about it. Can't waste any time. You nod. Smile a little.

Yes, I do.

I nod back. Grin. At last. It's a relief. I sink inside. Melt a little. Exhale. Breathe like it's the best thing.

Perfect, I say.

Is it?
Yes.

***

We finish our drinks. You're on a timeline, you're going to another event. We move outside. We stand by the traffic, talk by the rickety ashtray on the wall. You smoke a vape. I tug on a Marlboro Light, look at you, lean in, find your mouth.

We kiss but it's fighty. I pull you. You pull me. It doesn't work.

There's a struggle. A misunderstanding. I open my mouth. You kiss me. You open your mouth. We try again. It's still a little testy. I hold your face, you smile, pull back, pull away.

I've got to go, you say.

I know.

We say goodbye. I kiss your hand. Help you with directions to London Fields. You start to leave. Swish away. I turn back towards home, walk a few paces, then I bump into a friend who's out for the night. He's dressed up, wearing loafers and splashes of cologne.

You're flushed, he says.

Tipsy, I say. Been on a date.

He hugs me.

Nice one.

You?

Off out. Gotta sink a few beers.

We hug again. I leave him, walk home a little wobbly. Evening rays follow me. I'm dazed but not overrun. Full of you. Femme. I get to my front door, stagger in, collapse on the sofa, dizzy, short of breath.

***

Our second date is at my apartment. We arrange it. My friend is still away.

You don't want to stay over, you want to go home. You tell me beforehand. It's prearranged.

We don't write a contract but we talk, offer up insights. You spend hours with me, in my bed, pinned to the mattress. Butterfly limbs. Fucked like an insect. My fist inside you. All four fingers and a thumb. I dunk in and out, out and in, as you suck at the air.

I spit on you. Your reach expands. I stretch you apart.

Good girl. Good, good girl.

You come twice. Verbose. Yelping. Your eyes bore into me. Irises dull as a noisette. Your cunt bone is white, your skin is pale as light, but against it, your tissue is pink. I find you sexy. Lying back. Freshly fucked and fucked up. I'm tickled by the way you speak formally. Cordially. A very good girl. And then you fuck like a maniac. Your nails rip at me.

Voracious. Daring, like the shadows in August. Pointy, like the scratch of a needle. Bitey, like the metal clamp on an areola. I feel cruel. Demanding. Bend you to my will. You submit well (surrender you later call it). I pin you on your back, don't flip you. You find the pillow freely. It never leaves your neck. I roll my inner arm over you. Teasing you. Skin to skin to skin. I slap your cunt. Go at it again. Break over you for hours. Work on you. Weave my way in. Before you leave, we stand in the patio. Watch the moon wax and wane. Fizzing with sex. Fizzing with sweat. Both bodies thrumming.

***

The next morning, I wake with eyes bolted. Send you a text. I write you things (this is always an indication of something profound). I write about our night, the fairy lights of moments stringing together, the sweep of your contradictions. About you being filthy but formal. You eat up my words. You like me, but you're busy. I hand you space. Leave a long leash. We don't speak for 5 days, then you pick up the thread, look at your texts. We make a third date. I propose to meet you outside. In the air and the light. In Victoria Park.

Let's count the Egyptian Geese, I say. Eat ice creams.

Amazing.

I'll assume the butch spirit. Throw down my jacket for us to lie on.
Cannot wait.

***

We meet by the cafe, near the lake, grab iced Kombucha in bottles. You kiss me on the mouth. Take my hand. You wear Birkenstocks. A black dress. We walk to a quiet spot. The grass breaks like eggshells. There are families dotted around. Children. Dogs as swift as treacle.

We find a spot by the water. I wear a black boiler suit that I know you'll like. And you do. You say so. You always wear black. A gothic Dolly Parton. I lay down my jacket. You have a rug. A basket full of snacks. Kettle Chips, carrot sticks, grapes.

The water is close to us. There are long-legged birds that look like herons, but are egrets. There are Canada Geese. There are smaller birds with red beaks that may be coots.

I pop grapes, swig Kombucha, grin. You twist my hair in your fingers. Tug it. Lie back, tumble back, fall back. I hang over you. We kiss. It is full-lipped. Extended. Better than before.

I lie on you, lie against you, body to body. My cunt clutches yours. Slots in. I feel your pelvic bone mash me. Crumble against mine. I kick your legs apart. You lift your dress, clutch my arse. Exhale. We move like this. Your tits jiggle out of your dress, rise up either side, bob out. Your tits are small, shell-like, just how I like them. Your hair is raven. You laugh like a klaxon.

I bite into you, crack your skin, inhale you, exhale you. You gasp. Your hair sticks to you like paint.

Fuck, you say.

Yes. Where?

Touch me.

I roll off you. My legs are like scissor blades. You lift your dress further and nod. I see your knickers, grab them. They tear a little. I fetch my fingers in, against your cunt. It breaks open. Your lips are slippy. Liquid-like. I curl my fingers. They form tight as a blade, smooth as an onion.

I want to press deeper. You spread your thighs. I want you wide. I want to go in. I dunk my fingers, push in my nails, deep as my knuckles.

Inside. Relentless. Where I was before. In the park, toddlers run around. Wheelchair users with a couple of carers. My fingers click. Make sounds. Your lips puff up, bunch out, swell, blossom. I have to go in. Got to. The toddlers run away. You stop my hand.

Let's go back to mine.

Bus? I say.

Uber.

You slide your knickers over. Drop your dress. I grab my jacket. We scramble our things together. You fetch up the rug, the grapes, the Kombucha. I'm shaking. My fingers smell of you. Wet. Curled up. Your cunt is open, rounded. We barely straighten our clothes. My dick is alive in my boiler suit. Fiery, like a million red ants. Hungry, like the last gasp of appetite. Eager to enter you. Like a chisel is eager to bust rock. My arse is buckled by muscle clenches, tendons, nail scratches. I feel desperate. Not frugal. You are heavily distracted. Fist-hungry, wide-eyed, horny.

Over ready to have me please you (as I am over ready for you to please me).

***

We walk across the park. Egrets skim the water. Egyptian Geese scatter. Wings of grey, wings of orange, wings of tan. I watch you walk to the road. Book an Uber. We stand together. Hand in hand. My fingers pulse with blood. Your flesh still sings around me. We smile. Press wrists. I'm buckled up, dick-heavy, handsome. Broken by the prospect of you. Scored by a million nail stings. Your face is a peony. Dull pink. Open, restless, young.

***

I'm older than you by so many numbers. 57 to your 32. A whole calender swoops around us.

Year by year.

Day by day.

Night by night.

Week by week.

Minute by minute.

Season by season.

Butch/Femme.

D/S.

Good Girl/ Bad Daddy.

25 years against our frames.

You do the counting, you went to maths' club. That's 2+5+7+11. A sequence of primes. A primary placement. Against you and against me. Showing what we are and what we will be.

I want all of it, all of it, all of it now. In an avalanche of orgasms.

2

Untitled, May 13th by Ma Bo

It's summer before summer.

The buds have yet to bud, the thought of budding yet to form inside the wood. Boughs and twigs like lifeless bones, gnarly and naked and about to snap. The air is not dressed with the sugary scent of sap stirring beneath the bark. But with the square spice of the fir, the pine, and the spruce, their needles prickling the blue sky.

You have never seen such a blue sky. This blue sky folds inwards into the river, creasing and making an horizon. There are no corners in this northern landscape, an unmarked bight, but one carved into that rock stowed behind a bigger boulder, hidden from view of highway 138. Highway on which he is trudging forward in his white car.

At once, he pulls over. Maybe to pee, maybe to grab a bite in the trunk of his car. Maybe to think. It does not matter. It is by chance that he stumbles upon this unmarked bight, tucked away. He bats his lashes, taking in the soft sand, beige and darker where it touches the earth, and the burnt orange and shell pink rocks, and the white stitched water, cornea clear.

He pulls over closer and parks down the hill from the highway, in a bed of dry grass. He cracks the windows open and turns the engine off. The engine vibrations hush down to a whisper. Then stop.

Strolling down, he notices the sun. Oddly a summer sun. High and utter, blazing upon all angles. It is nearly noon. His shadow does not follow him on the beach. He strolls alone, unsplit. The sand simmers and not quite burns the palm of his feet, as he walks barefoot, his shoes dangling from his hands. Behind him his trace soon trails off into the quivering heat waves, a mirage-like skin hovering close to the ground.

He climbs over the big boulder now, which shoulders smaller ones, a limb of rocks decaying into a point. Among these rocks is the corner, where he sits. He lays his leather coat down and sits. He listens. To the clambering thunder of the occasional traffic. The gentle breathing and sloshing of water. The quiet breeze ruffling his hair, billowing his clothes, and inviting him to undress.

He stands up. He peels his layers like an artichoke, down, down to the heart. Every time the traffic strikes, for the fraction of a thought, his hand suspends its motion. Then he finishes folding his clothes neatly, piling them right there, except for his jeans overalls, which he sets at arm's length. At last, he sits again, nude.

The tide had begun to ebb, baring wet sand and clusters of barnacles and tufts of glossy varech. The lapping of water feels erotic, thinking about the slow-burn erosion is erotic, beseeching him into lust.

Lust rocks in the hollow of his pelvis, a basin not yet overflowing. A blush. Tilting his head back, he spreads the wing-span of his thighs, feet at a square angle. The water licks the velvety sea grass, bright green, that coats the lower rocks like fur, and the air licks the pubic hair that runs down his legs, wriggling like antennas. He then gapes his vulva and takes the sun in his four-lipped mouth. Wedged in his corner like that, he ripes and rots, sap and honey pooling.

His musk and the low tide's sulphurous scent whirl in eddies of wind.

The basin threatens to spill. What if a truck pulls over? What if the trucker hurries downhill and past the boulder for a quick wee? In his late forties, bald, chest hair puffing out the collar of his shirt, dark and curly, as is the bush shrouding his penis, and that he can peek at through the trucker's fly opening. The trucker pulls back his foreskin, uncovering the pink head. A stream of urine spurts out.

He lifts his gaze and meets his, who has been watching, still. A puddle of water.

The stream of urine halts, interrupted by the trucker's sudden erection. He blinks. His hand on his penis tries to tuck it back into his pants, unsuccessfully. He glances at his erected flesh. When he looks back up, in his direction, he has moved. He has moved slightly. A finger has pulled back his hood, and his swollen knob protrudes, a greedy slug. His half-closed eyes meet his, wide open. He half-nods at him, petting a timorous animal, bidding him to step closer. And closer. And closer.

When the trucker is close enough for him to hear the air coming in and out through his nose, which he has flat, and his cheeks flushed, a moan foams in his throat. He heaves a sigh. The heat congests him. The trucker strokes his hardness near, so near. Almost. Not yet. He moans. His tailbone embeds itself in the rock while his hips rotate open, more open, and the small of his back arches skywards. His lust is pressurised from the thousands of miles of rocks beneath him. Lips parted, he pushes two fingers on his tongue, warm, wet, then, like throwing a pebble down a cliff, down his throat, not breaking eye contact with the trucker.

A precum pearl rolls onto his taste buds. The trucker took the last step, stepping into the corner, a foot on his right, a foot on his left, his groin levelled with his mouth. At first he puts down his glans, fully roused from his sheath, berry red, at the centre of his tongue. He lifts it, barely an inch, to stroke it. The tongue stretches further, the uvula pulsates. He puts it back down, then slowly lodges it, inch by inch, down the throat.

The throat opens, mucus and saliva. Until he can't breathe. He pauses there. He feels the tightness. He waits.

Gripping his waistband with one hand, he pulls him inside his voice, up to the hilt. The penis hardens, harder. His pubic hair smells like sweat and rust. His other hand teases his slit, overflowing, and his knob, congested. What the trucker does to his throat, opening and poking, he can feel deep in his crotch. The basin cracks. His hips rock, his nipples perk up. The trucker pulls out, curved and slimy. Strings of saliva attach to his chin. He begs him to fuck him. Please, please fuck me, he says. On all fours. He obeys, eager. The trucker thrusts himself into him, his fleshy self impaling him. Open your cunt, boy. He does so, obediently. He loves to obey. He loves to lust in pleasure, and that pleasure to be wielded by the trucker like clay. Dirty and moist and plastic clay.

Precariously, he grasps the round humps of his ass with both hands, pulling them apart. The trucker groans. The anus is closed and alive, twitching. The trucker spits on it and rubs the spit with his thumb. The anus yields. The thumb, short and thick, is eaten hungrily, and briskly he whines. He feels the thumb pressing down the hard cock in his vagina, orienting the tip which now hits that spot. That acute and dazzling spot. The pit. He wails. Yes, fuck. Fuck yes. Right there. Fuck me right fucking there.

The trucker cums in a few strokes. Then, uninterrupted, he pees. He empties what was left of his bladder. He fills him to the brim and more. And more. He pulls out, and the semen and the urine gush out, hot and sticky and bitter trickling down his fuzzy thighs. The anus's pupil round open, letting light inside flesh.

His eyelids part open. He closes them again, blinded by the sun. High and utter. He blinks the blindness away. Wedged in his corner, his legs spread wide apart, feet at a square angle, he touches his tumefied vulva. He did not cum yet. Almost. Not yet. Ripe and rotten folds of flesh. The true self is the pit. Here to take root, to take water, to take sun.

What if a biker gang pulls over?

Two fingers reach into the flesh. He fucks himself enthusiastically, palm squelching against the pubis. His fingers reach for the pit, aroused and raw, and he feels his entrails melt as the bikers skewer him. Vigorous arms hold him up and open as they take turns fucking him, cumming in his cunt and fucking the cum into scum. They smell of leather and mink oil. What a whore, they say. Highway 138's cum dump, aren't you? We are all fucking you, bad boy. Bad, bad boy. He gags, and they slap him across the face. He perks his butt and jerks his head back, panting and tearing up.

Four fingers are now stretching him. Behind his teeth, his tongue is wide and his breath ragged. He is straddling two bikers whose cocks are double penetrating him, he feels like he could break in half. His walls are caving in on them. Almost, almost. A third biker gropes his breast and pinches the nipple. Acutely. Muscles twitching, mind blank—he hatches, cumming hard and loud. Like lightning.

He squirts a little river, quivering, sighing, his hand flat and strumming the vulva back and forth, releasing the cyprine waters.

All at once the flood dwindles, and the blush he felt in his crotch, a sunset blush, wilts into a bruise, purple and tender.

His water trickles down the rock, finding its way in and through the cracks, irregular. With what agency but its own. Down, down to the river, to be part of the river, becoming the river.

When you see the river again, when you think "river" upon seeing the river, you will hold in thought, in an intimate crease of your mind, unbeknownst to you, his cyprine.

That pleases him. Unfolding his clothes, he slides back into the fabrics. Clothed at last, heading back to his car, he walks next to his steps imprinted in the sand. He pauses a minute, crouching down, holding briefly in the clasp of his attention a tuft of tiny flowers, their purple bells cupping the sun. Saxifrage, indeed. Spring has sprung.

3

Too Far To Touch by Nillin Lore

Eddie glanced around. Excitement and nervousness overcoming all of his senses as he neared the observation binoculars he and his girlfriend Cass had scouted out weeks ago.

They were a recent acquisition by the City of Saskatoon in its efforts to swiftly ramp up tourism through whatever means possible, which in this case supposedly meant some telescopic eyesights mounted on pivots and poles. Set up at various points along the Saskatchewan River, each station allowed tourists and locals alike to observe the influx of pelicans visiting the city's weir every summer.

Only, Eddie wasn't here for the pelicans.

Weeks of careful planning with Cass and their mutual friend Marshall, was finally going to pay off. They had all purposely waited for a day exactly like this. No-one in the secret trio was busy with work or other obligations. It was a quiet evening along the river trails, just rainy and windy enough to persuade everyone else to stay inside. Exactly what made it the perfect time for Eddie, Cass and Marshall to be there.

Peering through the binoculars they'd settled on, Eddie scanned the treeline across the river from him. The sun was only just starting to set, its stunning orange light mixing with the cloudy skies to create a dreamlike sepia tone that made the scenery look like an old photograph.

After a couple of moments he found what he was looking for. There, just deep enough off the walking paths among the foliage to not be easily visible unless you were looking very carefully, stood Cass and Marshall. They were both positively beaming with excitement, practically bouncing where they stood.

Once he was sure there was nobody nearby, Eddie reached into his pocket, unlocked his phone and dialed Cass' number. Through the binoculars he could see Cass smile and do a happy little hop. She had carefully thought out her outfit, which consisted of a pair of warm black fleece leggings and her favorite brown, blue, and white striped ragg wool hoodie jacket with a zip up front. Both were enough to keep her warm while also making her body easily accessible for play. She tapped Marshall on the shoulder and pointed in Eddie's direction, then raised her own phone to her ear.

"Eddie! Can you see me, baby?" she asked.

"Yeah, I can see you, hun." Eddie responded.

Marshall was already kissing Cass along her neck and shoulders, a detail that he could faintly hear through the phone as he watched it happen through the binoculars.

A quick pang of jealousy hit. Not that he wasn't excited about what was to come, but a part of him always felt a little bit nervous and insecure watching his girl playing with somebody else. The moment quickly passed and he settled in to watching and enjoying the show.

"Good! Remember, no touching yourself. At all." Cass explained in a cute, yet matter-of-fact tone. "You can only watch. But when we're done, I'll take care of you and all of that pent up energy, okay?"

"Okay." Eddie affirmed, his cock already throbbing and twitching in his pants.

"And Eddie, I love you."

"I love you too Cass."

With that, they both hung up. Eddie let out a deep sigh of arousal as he watched Cass put her phone back into her pocket and begin to passionately kiss Marshall who immediately went to unzip her hoodie.

Her tits looked amazing, as usual. Eddie noticed the shiver of excitement that caused her upper body to subtly twitch as the cool air ran over her fully exposed chest. Marshall cupped his hand around one of her petite, round breasts. His fingers teasing and squeezing Cass' already hard nipple.

Cass tilted her head back and let her mouth drop open giving Marshall the means to kiss down the front of her neck and between her breasts before licking and sucking on her sensitive nipples. She arched her back, losing herself in the throes of lust while Marshall slowly lowered himself to first one knee, then the other, his lips worshiping her cute stomach as he went. His fingers curled under the waistline of her leggings, tugging on them playfully as he licked along the upper ridges of her pubic hair.

Marshall tugged Cass' leggings to her knees, fully exposing her nicely trimmed pubes and smooth girl dick.

Eddie could tell that being outside was having quite the effect on her. She was already partially hard when Marshall hungrily took her into his mouth.

It took every ounce of self-control for Eddie to ignore his own erection that was now pressed firmly, and a little uncomfortably, against his tight jeans. He awkwardly shifted his hips hoping to find a more comfortable placement, but more than comfort he wanted to feel *pleasure*. The thought of pulling his own cock out to stroke right then and there crossed his mind. Cass' instructions and fear of arrest were all that kept Eddie from giving in to those sudden urges.

In place of outright masturbating, he instead relished in the sensation of his own thighs and the fabric of his clothes rubbing against his cock while he squirmed in place.

Meanwhile, oblivious to Eddie's desperate horniness, Cass gripped a handful of hair on the back of Marshall's head as he bobbed up and down on her. Panting, she caressed her smooth stomach, and traced her fingertips up to her breasts to play with them while working her hips to fuck Marshall's mouth.

After a moment she licked her lips and reached into her pocket, pulling her phone out once again. Seeing this, Eddie instinctively reached for his cell without taking his eyes from the binoculars. It hardly had time to ring before he answered.

"I'm here, baby. I'm still watching."

"Oh my god, Eddie. It feels so fucking good. I want you to hear me cum. Can you hear me?" she asked, her voice quivering through her gasping breaths.

"I can hear you. God you look so fucking hot, Cass."

"I'm so close, Eddie. I'm so close. Oh fuck... fuck, Eddie! Baby, watch me! I'm going to cum!"

To his surprise, Cass' phone was picking up a lot of sound. Even with her moans and panting breath, Eddie could also make out the wet gagging that immediately followed each thrust Cass made of her full length down Marshall's throat.

"Do it! Fill his goddamn mouth, hun." Eddie whispered loudly, careful to not yell just in case somebody walking by might overhear him. He could feel that his boxers were now damp with pre-cum, his cock felt sore from how hard it had gotten.

Cass' voice cracked as she cried out. Her bare thighs quivering in Marshall's firm grip, her body lurching forward in small spasms. She looked down, laughing as she attempted to catch her breath, then addressed her playmate while Eddie continued to watch and listen.

"Look at me, Marshall. Open up and show me."

There was a pause, then a happy giggle.

"Good boy! Now swallow it for me."

Marshall stood up in the distance, wiping his mouth with the sleeve of his jacket. He pulled up Cass' leggings and began to zip up her jacket, all without being asked. Eddie, now content with the show, started the awkward walk back to his car whilst being careful to conceal his erection under his jacket. It helped with hiding his arousal, but also made it easier for him to tease himself through his jacket pocket.

He smiled as Cass caught her breath over the phone.

"How was that, baby? Did you like it?" her voice was soft and soothing, and yet, Eddie could hear a hint of anxiety, likely out of worry for his feelings.

"It was absolutely incredible, Cass." he assured her, and he meant it too.

"I love you so much, and I loved watching you… but I don't think that I'm going to be able to wait until we get home."

After everything he had just witnessed, all he wanted now was to have his turn to play outside as well.

"Alright, be quick but please drive safe, my love. This time we can have Marshall watch us."

Cass' voice betrays her shift into submissiveness more than she probably would have liked. Eddie always could tell. He genuinely appreciated that she was as much of a switch as he was, especially in moments like this. By the tone of her voice, Cass was desperate for him to absolutely fuck her brains out, and he was more than happy to bend her over against a tree to show Marshall how it's done.

4

I Spy by Cash Torn

The old truck's clock informs me we have three hours of driving to go. In the passenger seat, my boy is fast asleep. We rose at 5am to beat the Sydney traffic and summer heat. This boy is not an early riser. He cannot drive manual, which is one reason Daddy drives. But boys don't get free rides. His job, is to keep me entertained.

Late morning sun beams through the windows, warming his skin and illuminating his face, reddening the brown in his hair and beard. His mouth hangs slightly ajar, contented snoring noises emanating with the rise and fall of his chest. Just looking at him, hunger rises within me. The desire to sink my teeth into him and devour his perfect softness is immediate.

The sleeves from his t.shirt were ripped in a fitful rage last heatwave. A 40 degree celcius decision where discomfort from humidity trumps any discomfort of strangers seeing your top surgery scars. I trace my fingers along the scar's edges into the dark nest of armpit. I can feel his sweat from the Australian summer and exertion from packing the truck. My dick is instantly hard.

I dislike my boys wearing deodorant. I love the smell of sex and testosterone. He resisted at first, so many years of social conditioning. But he is a good boy. Eager to please. Eager to offer himself to me as I like. Now, his pits remain perfectly untarnished.

Eyes on the road, using his scar as a map, I trace my fingers to nipple. I squeeze and his innocent eyes open, blinking himself back from sleep into the passenger seat.

"Sir?"

"You've neglected your duties boy."

I pinch his nipple harder and there is a sharp inhale.

I slide my hand down to his sports shorts. Thin and elasticated for easy access. I caress the fur on his stomach before lifting the waistband and placing my hand above his dick. It pleases me greatly that he is without underwear.

His eyes are closed again, hips thrusting intuitively. He is desperate for his little prick to be closer to me. I gently stroke his pubic hair, his inner thighs, around his dick, below his dick. His sweet moans make me smile.

"I spy, with my little eye, something beginning with S."

He looks at me in confusion, wriggling in his seat. Yearning eyes of brown and green meet my steely blue as I grip his shorts in my fist.

"Something. Beginning. With S."

I wink at him. Play along boy.

"Ohhh, uh. Is it a Signpost Daddy?"

"Nice guess boy, but the correct answer is Slut. Now, take off your shirt."

There are no vehicles in front or behind and I utilise this chance to take all of him in. His hands stop squeezing chipped brown leather and rise to the hem of his homemade muscle tee, lifting it up and over his head in one fluid movement. Arms raised, I can see dark ringlets in his pits from sweet perspiration. More curls in the glorious fur across his chest and stomach. A single drop of sweat skis off piste down the curve of his lat muscle and my body thrums with scalding desire and thirst. The offending garment is discarded inside out at his bare feet, amongst forgotten coffee cups and crumbs.

"I spy, with my little eye, something beginning with B."

He smiles confidently and points to himself.

"Boy!"

"Wrong!"

I snap the elastic at his waist with a jolt and nod at the remnants of breakfast in the cup holder.

"Banana skin. Now, lose the shorts."

He is grinning at me, I am looking at the road but I can feel it. He places both hands on mine, on his stomach. He strokes my paw before hooking his thumbs under his waistband. I glance from road to his crotch and back. Each time I return, the fabric has descended ever so slightly further. I fucking love a tease.

The sexual tension in the cab is thick and electric. The sky above is clear expansive blue but the air in the truck tastes of tropical thunder storms. Senses on high alert, vision sharpening, I watch the boy undress as I steer my trusty Ford with the shuddering suspension. The vibrations are an extra bonus. Shorts nudge past his crotch, his hardness now visible through the pelt between his thighs. I can smell his hot hole and my dick is charged with need. I adjust my pants to accommodate my swelling.

We ride in silence for an obscene and immeasurable time as the last of his clothes make their way down his thighs. Passed fading bruises from last night and the night before, until he sits smugly in his naked glory, leaning back against the window, legs ajar so I have a view of the treasure between them.

"I spy. With my little eye. Something, beginning, with C."

He laughs that mischevious laugh that is solely for my ears. Throwing his hands up in faux frustration he makes an exaggerated show of rolling down the window and hanging out to look for the elusive C word.

"I don't know Sir!"

His delicious furry butt makes a satisfying slap as he chucks himself back onto worn leather.

"A cockatoo?"

I slam on the brakes, causing him to grip the door to hold fast. Making a sharp right turn into a smaller road, momentum pushes him deeper into his seat.

"I know how much you love a cock or two."

Grinning, I reach over and snap open the glove box. Inside is a girthy seven inch silicone piece and full bottle of lubricant. Staring ahead, I place my cock between his thighs, close enough to drive him wild, but not near enough to actually touch. I squeeze a mighty dollop of lube into his crotch sending his senses into overdrive. He is panting now, as a deer should when faced with a wolf.

I nudge towards his swollen, dripping trans dick. Grazing him, I slide in and out, tapping his sensitive tip and he bucks helplessly. His eyes are closed and he is biting his lip. No thoughts now, only desire. My gorgeous plaything. His gasps intersperse with guttural moans and incoherent whispers. Beads of sweat form amongst his chest hair. I take my eyes from the road to watch a droplet swell and rush between his pecs towards shining abdominal fur. He lifts himself, hovering and watching, desperate for permission to sit on the toy, to ride it.

"Please?"

I shake my head and make another quick turn which propels him back to seated position, silicone nestled infuriatingly against his sopping hole and throbbing manhood.

The movements make my boy's eyes flick from side to side, finally taking in the surroundings outside the vehicle. Reality hits him like Daddy's favourite heavy padddle.

"Are we in a town Sir?!"

I have slowed the truck from motorway speed to accommodate our new terrain. It is indeed a town. To our left there is a school and a church. To the right, a pub and a grocery. We are driving so slowly I could make eye contact with locals on the street, of which there are many.

"Open your legs."

I sense the conflict tense within him, being naked and wanting and so close to the public. Still, he is my good, obedient boy and after a beat, he acquiesces.

I slide the lubed up cock all over him now, mixing his wetness with the bottled stuff. Down and up from dick to front hole and back again, teasing every soaked and anguished nerve ending in his groin. His body begs for more, pumping and pushing himself against the silicone as his face presses against the window, panting *oh fuck oh fuck oh fuck.*

"You're being so good for Daddy. My favourite fuck toy. My perfect little slut. No-one outside can even tell what a desperate hungry hole you are."

His moaning intensifies with praise. All he wants is to please me. We stop at a junction and I carelessly slap his prick and hole.

"Oh God, oh shit, oh fuck!"

I know his body better than he knows it himself. He will come when *I* want him to come. He has no choice in the matter.

"This town is small boy and we're halfway through it. Can you see the next traffic lights ahead? After them, it's back to the motorway. You better hope we don't stop next to a truck bigger than this one though. The driver could look right in at you, all naked and wet. Now, hold this."

I push the dildo inside him and his eyes bulge. He squeezes his thighs together to hold the pleasure inside and crosses his feet to keep it secure. Taking my hand back, I wipe excess lube on his thigh before shifting gears and setting off, eyes fixated on the lights ahead. Green just now but I know they will be red for us, for what comes next.

I return my hand to the base of the cock. My boy's legs relax, his hole submits to me and I am fucking him. Slipping inside of him over and over, pounding myself into his sex. Knowing him from the inside. Building rhythm in the way that will keep him on the edge.

"Oh Daddy! Oh fuck! Oh Daddy!"

I love how vocal he is and the squeals are shifting to a frantic pitch. Almost to the point of no return. His arms flail. One hand grabs the roof of the cab, the other clutches seat. If anyone looked in at us now, we could not deny the scene. Two tranny deviants, fucking ferociously.

We are almost at the junction and with every thrust inside my boy I telepathically demand the lights switch from green to red.

At the last millisecond, green descends to amber and I slam on the brakes, unclick my seatbelt and finally reach him with both hands. Holding his throat I bite his lower lip as he spasms and howls in my grip. We have just enough time before the lights turn again.

I lift his arm and shove my face into the damp curls, breathing him in. His scent makes me feral. His pits smell like his man-cunt; heady, intoxicating. I snort greedily, inhaling huge lungfuls of him. His essence crosses my blood brain barrier and alters my neuro-chemistry, like snorting a fat line of cocaine.

I lick rhythmically in time to his whimpering, devouring his sweetness, consuming him as he fucks himself with my cock between his legs. Between mouthfuls, I ask if he's ready?

"Oh fuck please Daddy?! Please? Please?!"

I have managed such restraint until this time. He is begging and squealing, no choice but to orgasm at my behest, because he is mine. His flesh is my celestial sustenance and my teeth sink fast between older yellow bruises on his chest. My free hand slaps his dick like a metronome. Shouting and shuddering through *le petit mort* I growl with the satisfaction of meat between my jaws and the sprays released with each strike upon him.

Breathing slows and I release the power from my maw. The aftershocks ripple through him and I want him to ride the lightning as far as he can go. Holding his quivering junk in my hand I whisper gentle reassurance in his ear.

A sudden HONK disturbs the orgasmic bliss. The traffic lights are green and cars behind us are pissed.

My beautiful boy waves a limp wrist out the window in a faggy show of thanks to the honking driver. I survey the passenger side debris with glee. His squirt is everywhere, soaking the clothes at his feet, spraying the windscreen and combining with lube to create a sloshing puddle in his seat.

Grinning, I throw the truck into first and speed off, back towards the motorway.

5

Stripped by Christian Pan

The sound of your door slamming shut punches me back to consciousness.

How long was I out?

I yawn, stretch, then peer beyond the smudges peppering the glass of my window on the passenger side and take in the world beyond. Shafts of light the color of gold and fresh blood paint the branches of so many birch trees that I can't even count them. Their slender bark-covered trunks form a perfect perimeter of privacy around this wide grassy clearing. Everything is alive and vibrant here, so much so that my eyes start to well up with tears. Too much beauty, all at once, always makes me cry.

I need to get out of the city more.

I step out of the car, then fast walk to catch up with you.

Blades of crushed green grass leave a trail for me to follow. I watch your strong backside stride straight as an arrow towards the trunk of an old tree, a weathered magus amidst the other fresh and interchangeable saplings. Its wide trunk stretches upwards, its branches twisting like arms writhing above in petrified longing.

Without you needing to utter a single word, I understand why you insisted we come *here* for my first time. In every myth, the virgins are taken somewhere sacred before the blood is drawn.

Finally catching up to you, I stand and wait a few paces behind your strong broad back. The air kisses my face coldly as the sun's yolk disappears behind the trees, and unseen cicadas begin playing their evening nocturne. Your chin gently nods up and down. I imagine your smile. Inhaling, my nostrils flare, then sense a distant hint of kerosene and burning oak on the wind.

Out of habit, I pull my mobile phone from my pocket. I know better than to take a picture of *you*; I know how much you hate these things. Phones, internet, devices, just different names for the same kind of poison, ruining our ability to communicate, to be close to each other, to feel.

I just wanted a picture of that old oak there in the clearing. Not to post anywhere. Just for me. So I could remember.

Before my handheld machine comes between me and the real world, your giant hand wraps around my wrist.

Look, you tell me. *Don't just glimpse.*

I nod, my cheeks splotched from the blood pounding from my heart. You take my phone and tuck it inside your front pocket. Meanwhile, I try to *look*.

The trees.

The grass.

The lingering traces of light from the setting sun.

The world is beautiful—of course—but also unsettling. I think about how far away we are from the city, from people, from everything familiar. Even though I am *in* the natural world right here, I feel isolated.

That's so fucked up.

Yet: the fear and the approaching night and these beautiful trees, they're also conspiring to really fucking turn me on. Which is the whole reason why we're here.

Let me see you stripped down to the bone.

Your voice lilts into half-song, quoting one of my favorite tunes. What you ask feels dangerous. Images of various scenarios enter into my mind, but it's all a jagged pastiche, a film crudely spliced together from pieces of memory and hidden fantasies. My cock grows hard within my thin cargo pants, my flesh pressing firm against the front of the fabric.

Let's go. Help me get set up.

You briskly march back towards the car. Your shift in mood is abrupt and sharp like the language of your body. At the trunk, I upturn my forearms as you load me with gear: a long olive-colored tent bag and the food and beverage cooler. You prepare to carry the sleeping bags and mini-grill. Then, from behind the left wheel well, you grab a small bag made from black leather, and stuff it into the front of your belt. I don't remember us packing that alien object before we left the city. I'm about to ask you what's inside when you cross your index finger over the line of my lips.

Uh-uh, you say. *That's for later.*

*

Later, night bloomed across the blue above like a fresh bruise.

You had instructed me to find kindling. I returned happy as a puppy, a pile of dry twigs and small branches discovered along the treeline, close to where you gazed so intently earlier. As we rub our hands near the dancing flames, your eyes keep looking there, as if listening for a sign.

Are there any wild animals here? I ask.

You mean, besides us?

I stand, shake out the pins and needles from one sleepy leg, and look up above. The stars shine brighter here; in the city, they can barely breathe due to the light pollution. I feel closer to the cosmos here, as if I am seeing them for the first time. My eyes flood with water again. Too much beauty. I blink the tears away, and try. I want to remember this moment, not look away.

When I look at you again, your smile grows wider. I am reminded once again of how much I adore you, how much I need you. Who else would take me here, give me the gift of this place? Who else would baptize me?

Let's go, you say. *It's time.*

You brush away the dirt from your ass, and extend your hand to help me rise. You lead us away from the fire and our small camp, and toward the darkness close to the tree line. I hear nothing but my heartbeat pounding in anticipation, blocking everything else out.

The strength of your hand squeezes mine, and gives me confidence to do what will come next. What I asked you to do for me and to me. We stop by the old tree, and you tell me to remove my clothes. I do so calmly, quietly, knowing that this is part of the ritual, just like removing my phone earlier was part of the divestment. I stand naked, my erect cock extending forward from my loins, and can practically feel the soft light of the distant campfire behind you licking my skin.

Your silhouette instructs me to place my bare back up against the rough bark of the tree, then extend my arms behind me. I just fit around the trunk of this old wizard, and my eyes widen when you free the leather bag from your waist and toss open its flap. From its depths, you remove a length of zip cord and fasten it to my wrists. Within less than a dozen heartbeats, I am completely bound to this tree, naked.

My freedom and life rests literally within your hands. Without you, I would surely die out here. Unable to survive through the night's cool temperature or whatever nocturnal animals might be roaming here. My cock swells even further, engorged by the fear and the reality of my total submission. I love you, and the feeling is so strong that I want to weep again. I try to hold myself back, but I know that I am getting close.

Metropolis, you say–sing, *has nothing on this, eh?*

Returning to stand in front of me, my exposed body arches towards you, seeking contact. My vulnerable skin scrapes across the rough edges of the tree. I feel like St. Sebastian, my flesh writhing in ecstatic agony in anticipation of the next brutal shaft to pierce the skin.

And then it comes. I know it's coming. I've *begged* for it.

Your hand emerges from the leather pouch again, revealing the butterfly knife, the one you bought for me, specifically for tonight. Your wrist executes a swift series of flicks and twists, freeing the blade from its silver handle, catching the light from the fire behind you in blurred flashes. You hold the knife vertically now, letting me gaze about its sharp length, then slowly walk towards me, the steel mere inches from my skin.

Let me hear you crying just for me, you croon softly, almost a whisper. I nod, scared and aroused. You turn the blade horizontally in front of my lips, its blunt edge in front of my bottom lip.

Spit, you command.

I gather my spit up into the back of my throat, then pucker my lips to pour the thick saliva along the length of the steel. You add some of your own too, and you allow me to see our drool ooze off its surface before you lower the knife to my groin. When I feel the flat end of the blade along my stiff cock, I inhale sharply. It's warm.

You don't move the weapon lightly pressed against my flesh, choosing instead to patiently allow gravity to transfer the slobber from the knife onto my cock.

After endless broken cycles of breath, you raise the blade again up to my chest, and use your other hand to stroke me, lathered in the lubricant of your mouth's hot wetness. You keep working my cock, as your silhouette shows me the knife again.

Careful, you say. *Try not to move.*

You wield the knife in your hand like a quill, pressing its razor sharp tip into the flesh just above my beating heart, painfully slow. Puncturing the skin is the hardest, and the agony lets out a whine. Keeping my bright eyes locked on your shadowy face, the droplets of blood slowly pouring down my pectorals only makes my cock stiffen in your other hand. You stroke me faster, while keeping the blade moving slowly cutting.

I yelp.

Almost done, you coo. *You're so beautiful.*

You move the butterfly knife like you are tracing the outline of a simple shape, a signature in microcosm: the first letter of your name, carved over my heart. In my mind's eye, I can see the shape being formed, and I sense that you are nearly finished. I am trying to restrain my loins from ejaculating too soon, but your other hand is working me faster now, almost in fury.

Ohhhhh god, I shout. *Fuck fuck fuck!*

Beautiful, you say.

When the head of the knife leaves my bloody flesh, my mind and body know that you are finished carving, and that is when I finally come. My jizz spurts into your palm like liquid pearls, my body arching and jolting away from the rough surface of the tree. My arms strain uselessly against the ties behind me, the zip cord binding my wrists tearing into my skin.

The pressure and the effort, as well as the orgasm, cause the blood to pump out of the fresh wound you've made against my flesh. Your mark. Your name. Dug into my body and into my consciousness, forever.

You bring your hand up from my groin, and bring it close to your mouth. Your tongue flashes out eagerly, like a predator that had lay waiting in the shadows before striking. You walk behind me, and the knife cuts through the zip cords like butter. My shoulders are sore, my breath is trembling, and my eyes are filled with tears. I have never felt more alive.

Slowly, you fold up the knife, then place it in one of mine, ritualistically curling my fingers around it.

Yours, you tell me.

You cover my fresh wound with your hand, and then for the first time since our arrival, gently kiss my lips.

We need to irritate this, you inform me. *To make sure it scars over clearly.* I nod. You gather my clothes up for me, and then offer your upturned palm. I accept.

Come with me.

We walk, side by side, back to the fire.

6

Redwoods by Sharon Penance

Without fail I think of her every spring, just as the cottonwood seeds start to float down from their beds, drifting lazily about on warm currents.

Nic had that same kind of saunter, a general disinterest in most things that I found wildly attractive. And by late April of our senior year, Nic and I had been dating for a while. Time held absolutely no meaning when we were together and I was lovesick on the idea of her. She was the first person who really balanced me and somehow, we both managed to let our guard down with one another. There was a depth to our relationship that I craved, the kind that doesn't come along often.

It was the weekend and we were headed out of the stifle of our small, boonie hometown. A trailhead at the edge of a seemingly endless wilderness housing the last known location of any of our things. The temperature steadily dropped as we walked and the still of the night had settled over me in a way that felt rude to disturb with conversation.

Nic must have felt the same. Neither of us said much on our way, and it wasn't long before we found ourselves standing between towering old growth giants. It seemed as if the world had stopped. There was soft quiet stretching out around us and I could feel the shift, the transcendence into something new as we stood in the center of all that holy.

Nic turned towards me with her familiar, impish half-grin and shaggy brown hair falling over her eyes, undoubtedly hiding the desire I could sense in her. She closed the short distance between us, pushing me back towards the trunk of a sizable Cedar. The rough of the bark caught against me, even through the thick pad of my jacket. Nic leaned in to kiss me and rested a hand on my collar bone, her fingers stretching up along the side of my neck.

How is it... how could it possibly be that in the middle of nowhere, in the middle of all this wild open, that she could still find a way to trap me? I could feel my quickening pulse beat into her palm as I pushed back against her. Nic ran a hand up into my hair, grabbing a fistful right at the scalp. My mouth fell open in surprise and she filled it.

Her kiss grew into a wide smile and her fist was on my face before I knew it, fingers digging into my skin. I could feel the calluses, rough on her fingers, trail down the slope of my jaw.

Nic buried her way under my layers, her hands somehow everywhere and so unbelievably cold. She shoved my bra over like it was nothing, taking a nipple between her fingers as the others found their way to the small of my back. I arched up into her, my lips at her neck, biting down in gentle rebuttal as the edge of her denim jacket collar scratched at my face. Those fingers closed down in a flash as she pulled and twisted, the meaning unmistakable. Nic drew me into her, still holding my body tight. I'd bend wherever she'd take me.

She pushed up the hem of my skirt and pressed into my thighs. God help me with a wandering hand butch. I could feel that my underwear was already embarrassingly soaked through...so much for any utility in them. I could have worn nothing at all.

She noticed. Of course she noticed. Her hand closed over my cunt and a low moan leaked through my lips. I couldn't help it.

"Good girl. Come on, let's go." Nic wasn't asking. There was a grit in her tone and a look in her eye that I knew all too well.

For a minute I thought she would fuck me right there, fixed tight between her and this aged old wood. I tried to shift a little but lost my footing and stumbled, pulling us both down. Nic was able to catch herself a little, smoothly positioning herself over me.

Her hips held me to the ground and the world came into focus as she watched me writhe under her. I felt breathless but steam rose from our lips up to meet the sky. Pinning my arms, she pushed my legs apart with her thighs. I closed my eyes and opened my mouth.

Yes.

Please.

There was nothing. Just the weight of her holding me to the ground. I exhaled and looked up, she was watching me intently and very clearly waiting. If nothing else, her sternness and patience lit me on fire.

She sighed in response, her eyes blazing against the darkness with want. "I need you to use your words." she told me.

Of course. Absolutely.

But how do I explain that I want ALL of her, everything she is to be contained inside of me. That I want her to break me down and grind me into the dirt.

"Yes. I'll use them."

Still nothing.

"Please Nic. ...Please?" I begged.

My voice broke on the last please. I needed her more than I needed anything. My body ached and she was a cure just coiled and ready, the absence unbearable.

She leaned in and kissed me, slow and glorious and I savored every drop of her. And as she continued I felt a whine start to build in the back of my throat. Her, measured and steady, fueling my growing desperation. I was lost in her, exactly the way she liked.

Just as I thought I might come with my own sodden lust sliding slowly down the curve of my ass, she pulled back. Without warning the full force of her open fist connected against my cheek. The sound rang out before the trees damped it, my skin and bones radiating.

The metallic sour of blood and earth slowly pooled together in the soft hollow of my cheek. I gasped, tilting my head a little to spit, but Nic turned my face back to her.

"No. Swallow." She instructed.

I did. God I loved her. I smiled a little as I licked my bottom lip, checking if it was still intact.

Nic made a small strangled noise as she watched, like a gasp and a grunt combined into one. I stared up at her and bit my lip.

Her face smashed into mine and I furiously tried to consume everything she had to give me. Her hips grinding into me, she moved one hand to hold my wrists neatly above my head. My skin began to bristle as her short nails clawed a path down my side, tearing at the band of my tights. She moaned as I met her lips, hungry for the taste of her.

"More." The sound and strength of my own voice surprised me. This was the space I thrived in, my reserve crashing down all around us.

Nic wasted no time in pulling the thin cotton from between my legs, her fingers plunging beyond the slick of my thighs, deep into my cunt as my hips rose up in rhythm. She worked a third finger in, then all her knuckles followed. She was swift and unforgiving.

I wrapped around her as she pushed her way inside, stretching me open. Bands of muscle strained and broke. I whimpered, riding the high, so impossibly, excruciatingly full, silently begging for the world to slow again as adrenaline coursed through me. Nic's grip on my wrists softened, all of her attention held inside me.

"More."

It was barely a whisper but there again, all the same - an ask, a demand, a simple plea. Nic responded beautifully, my shoulders slammed back down, her thrusts driving me into the ground. Pain flared across my entire body. Every part of me was incinerating. I watched the sky through the treetops, although I'm not sure I saw anything at all.

"Come for me, baby girl."

Nic was at my ear, her words unleashing my climax into the night. It was my complete undoing. Nic moved a dirt covered hand to my chin as I felt the veins in my neck strain, everything else smoldered and muted.

"Fuck - Whitney." Nic was breathing heavily. I felt the familiar blush burn across my cheeks and I grinned sheepishly, giving a little shrug from right down there in the dust. I had to turn a little to look at her. She stared back, that chestnut colored hair even more tousled than usual, falling over half her face.

Nic was one of those people who always looked effortlessly disheveled and put together at the same time.

I turned over, tracing my fingers lazily across her sweat dampened black cotton shirt. Nic exhaled slowly, the fall of her sternum led my fingers to wander. My hand trailed down to her belt, which I fumbled with. Her jean button and zipper were far easier to conquer.

"Whitney," Nic started, but then stopped.

"Please?" I looked up at her, a little exasperated. I didn't want to beg a second time, but I was desperate to bury myself into her.

I wound a hand through her hair, kissing her softly. There was a pine needle stuck in her dark curls that I pulled free while shifting to straddle one of her legs.

I started rocking, just a little. Just enough for my body to bounce. I leaned in to kiss her again but she caught me before I could. Hands on my shoulders, roughly pushing me back down.

I tugged at the belt loops and worked my way between her legs. I struggled to get her underwear down. I was much more used to being on my knees for this.

I bowed my head and devoured her. Nic moaned out a steady flow of unintelligible expletives, her hands held tight at my neck. She didn't hold back. Each thrust of her hips a painful reminder for my bruised cheekbone. My tongue gently wrapped around her, and I waited.

Nic grabbed the back of my skull, pressing me into her. I couldn't breathe, but I didn't care. Soft gurgles caught in the back of my throat. It was blissful to be used in this way. The sound of my smothering alone setting us both on edge.

The gurgles gave way to something more urgent and I could feel Nic start to tense. I tried to look up at her as my chest burned, grabbing her hips as if it was somehow possible to get more of her. Her body heaved as she came, all of her pulsing and alive.

I stayed on her, holding motionless for her approval to change positions. I felt Nic's grip ease as cool air filled my lungs. Drool poured from my lips forming little puddles on the ground. I watched it stream, completely transfixed as I took in deep, ragged breaths. Nic's hand gently cupped my face, commanding my attention, and I somewhat clumsily crawled back up into her arms.

Somewhere close by, our friends were howling at the moon. Their drunken laughter filling the empty dark. Smoke swept through the trees. We'd have to collect ourselves at some point and find them, but I just wanted to be here a little bit longer. I curled my body into hers, fully spent and nestled in, ready to look for stars.

7

Concrete and Flames by Mx Slate Ruins

Jean jacket, corduroys, and a stiff cock in my strap. I'm seventeen and ready for a thrill. I feel naive, and yet knowing, all in the same breath. Flickers of light through the concrete. Boisterous laughter around the bonfire.

I know the depth of risk I'm taking and it terrifies me, but I need this.

It's a typical Friday night, the high school misfits have built a bonfire out of wood scraps and cardboard from cases of beer. I see the usual faces around the flames. It's not my crowd, but I've had some fun times here, being the token queer. Making out with the drunk girls trying to impress their boyfriends with queerness. It's a cheap thrill, but not what I'm looking for tonight.

I'll grab a beer and see what trouble I can conjure up, deeper in the ruins. Rifling through loot piles from the evening's beer run, the best I can find is a Rolling Rock.

These beer runs have become part of the Friday night rituals. The cashier doesn't even bother trying to run after us, anymore. He knows the drill. A hoard of teens pile out of a hatchback and keep the engine running. We spread out into the store, one asks him questions to distract him while the rest of us fill our jackets with chips and grab all the beer we can carry as we run out the door.

Quick and dirty.

I wander off into the ruins with my Rolling Rock, stepping over broken bottles and rebar. Kicking debris to the side, I clear a space to sit and sip my beer. Fuck sitting with this hard strap digging into my thigh. It hurts, but I'll manage.

These concrete walls were here even before Washington was declared a state, before roads and railways. Even then, it was dangerous to be queer.

We've all heard stories about the insane asylum. About the lady who wandered out of her cell and into the woods in the middle of the night. All the locals know about her. They looked for her, but not very hard. When someone stumbled upon her remains, all that was left were broken bones, her long white hair, and her nightgown.

Just to my right, I can see the abandoned tool shed where rusted coffee cans and tobacco tins of human remains were found. Bodies piled into the ovens and chaotically divided up into whatever was available. They were brought here to be forgotten and they were discarded just as carelessly.

There's no protection here.

This place used to criminalize the queers. Enslave them to farm work and cut open their skulls to cure them of their disease. Poor souls convicted of the illness of being different. The families disowned them, denying their family name be known on a gravestone.

Lighting up a smoke, I let my thoughts wander. The stories of my queer ancestors swirl around me. I sense their presence. I can hear the frogs calling into the autumn air. The scent of late August blackberries overripe on the vine, sunburnt and shriveling.

A heavy wave of grief washes over me. My bones ache. The cacophony around the fire continues and yet, I feel a stillness surrounding me. Looking around, there's no sheet covered figure floating, no spooky outline of a spirit, but I know I'm not alone.

If I'd been born a hundred years earlier, this would have been my fate too. Sure, I'd do my best to make the most of it. Taking a moment to listen to the Robins and Swallows sing while milking the cows every morning. Soaking in the afternoon sunshine as I tended the garden.

But every day ends the same, confined to my cell and used by whichever night guard wanted their turn with my body.

I can imagine it all too well. I hear their voices.

The clank of glass beer bottles shifting on the ground alerts me that someone has followed me to this hideout. My attention is pulled back to the present to see this scruffy man appearing in front of me.

I gather myself, running my hand through my hair, adjusting my cock and dropping my cigarette butt. He's taller than me, so I find a bit of rubble to stand on to look him in the eyes without straining. He must be a college guy, by the looks of his beard.

His gaze is intense. I don't falter. I hold his stare, knowing my power.

Button by button, I slowly undo myself illuminated by moonlight, dropping my jacket beside me. A deep connection between our eyes, daring him to look away. He shifts on his feet.

His discomfort entices me.

I watch his hand cautiously travel to his groin, allowing me time to protest. I stand tall and give him a nod. His dick is pressed hard against his Levi's. He steps closer, narrowing the gap between us.

I place my hand on his shoulder and push him to his knees. He sets down his beer and looks back up at me, patiently waiting for permission. I nod and feel his cold hands unzipping my corduroys.

I want this.

First, his scratchy hairs brush against my softness, then his tongue slips into my epicenter. Where my earth meets my sky, slick and hard. I can feel the corners of his mouth curl up as he delights in my arousal. Vibrations of his moans on my cock. The concrete rubble of the insane asylum shifts beneath my feet. Heartbeat pounding in my piece and my T-dick simultaneously. He works my silicone shaft with passion and determination.

Holy fuck, bless this enthusiastic cock sucker.

I want more.

I grab him by a fist full of hair and pull him up to his feet, pointing to the remnants of a window across the way. He's a grungy older guy, and I have no business fucking around with him, but I can't help myself. This urge is driving me, compulsing me to take what I want.

Stepping over chunks of concrete and cans. It's tricky to navigate even when you haven't had a drink, but now in the dark, with a raging hard on, it's a real challenge. My scruffy fucker looks back at me when he reaches the window ledge.

With a steady hand, I turn him around and bend him over, jerking his jeans down, revealingly his supple ass. Tightening my strap, it's finally time to satisfy this urge I've been fantasizing about for years.

Dust from the rubble coats his thighs as I press my big stiff dick into him, gripping his jock strap. He gasps and arches his back as my thighs clap against his.

My lungs ache as I pant, filled with smoke from the bonfire and Marlboro Reds. His hole clenches around my veiny prosthetic. My hard silicone piece pressed against my T-dick, my cocks colliding and converging. His dick pinned down against the rough concrete, scraping against it with every thrust. Each impact of my body against his, smashing his cock again and again.

It feels so good, but I don't want to give him my load just yet. He's close.

I spit on his asshole and slide two fingers in. Fuck, I love the feel of a swollen prostate. I reach around and stroke the length of his dusty prick. The grit hurts, just how he likes it. Grunting and groaning in response. His urgency is right at the surface. I can taste it.

My hole aches to be filled but that dirty dick is a problem.

I stop stroking him and he grumbles in frustration. His eyes are pleading for more. My raised eyebrow tells him to be patient, it'll be worth the wait. I push him back onto a large slab of what used to be a wall, its angle and height are perfect for my cravings.

I spit on his filthy cock, grab the condom from my back pocket, split the wrapper open with my teeth and roll it down his stiff shaft. I love how he throbs in the palm of my hand.

My hand pressed on his chest, he leans back and I climb on top of him. My cock standing tall as I slide down onto his. He strokes me, feverish with desire as I use his body to my liking. He's so hard and thick, my front hole is burning from the stretch. Fuck, it feels so good. I deserve this pleasure. Riding his fuck stick hard and fast.

Sweat is dripping from my brows and the salt burns my eyes. Ripping my shirt and binder off over my head. I shove the binder in his mouth and push his face to the side, concrete imprinting on his cheek.

My chest is bouncing freely as I continue to claim his cock as mine. Harder and harder till I can't bear it anymore. My cum escaping me and covering him. I can feel his load fill up the condom inside me, his moans muffled by my binder.

With legs wobbling, I slide off his shaft, rip the condom off, and grip it tight, making him squirm and screech. He tries to pull away from me but finds himself trapped beneath the boot I've pressed into his chest. I love torturing his cock.

Miserably writhing beneath my grip. Spit and cum and grit circling the head. It's a delightful pain. His legs are trembling as his back arches and his stomach quivers. I pause for just a moment, allowing him to look up at me, look into my eyes.

I want him to remember the face of the trans guy that's owning his dick.

Our eyes lock and I quicken my pace. Stroking every inch of his grit covered, scraped skin erection. A blow to his balls with every stroke. I slip a couple of fingers into his ass and that does it. His entire body shakes and trembles as I pull another load out of him, from a place he's never been before.

Yanking my spit soaked binder out of his mouth, I kiss him hard as I buckle my corduroys. I step back to hand him his beer and shove my binder into my back pocket. Draping my jacket over my shoulder, I grab my Rolling Rock, and I'm gone.

Wandering deeper into the ruins.

8

Steadfast and True by Anna Sansom

The ancient granite slab had soaked up heat from the day and, as I lay on it, I felt patches of lichen tickling my exposed skin. I stretched my arms wide and my fingertips traced the cavity of a chiselled groove that ran the length of the rock.

"That was for collecting the blood," Tay casually remarked. "From the sacrifices." They took one of my feet in each hand, their long fingers looping around my ankles, gently positioning my legs so my thighs parted.

"That's right," Bree said, from the other end of the stone plinth. She raked her stubby fingers through my hair, before dabbing a drop of frankincense oil between my eyebrows. "Sheep and goats, probably. But you never know. These stone circles could have been used for all kinds of ceremonies and rituals. I doubt we are the first to do this." She placed her small hands on my bare breasts and inhaled loudly. "Breathe with me, baby."

I followed her command and, on the exhale, allowed my body to relax deeper on top of the stone.

"Good girl."

The summer's evening light was rapidly fading and when I turned my head to the side, I glimpsed the curved orange glow of the sun sliding below the horizon. We'd timed it perfectly. For a brief moment, my thoughts projected forward: how were we going to make it back? The walk here had been difficult for me, even with my walking poles and my two companions. We'd had to trek for about a mile, across lumpy fields and over a couple of stiles before we reached the clearing that held the remains of this special place. How was I going to manage that in the dark?

There should have been nine standing stones, Tay had told us when we arrived. The legend said that nine young women had danced naked on the hillside, the night before the Sabbath, to a tune played by the devil himself. When the sun came up and shone its light on the debauched scene, the women were turned to stone. Excluding the central horizontal slab that my naked body now lay on, there were only seven other stones visible.

"You and me make nine," Bree had told me.

"Does that make me the devil?" Tay had asked, with one eyebrow raised and a glint in their eyes.

It was Tay who'd chosen this place. Bree was in charge of the ritual. And me? Well, I was the one who'd asked for this to happen. It had been hard to admit that I felt like I was gradually losing myself. I had always been the dependable one. The strong one. The 'TNT friend' who would blow my friends out of any prison – whether incarcerated or self-imposed. The lover who gladly took control in a scene and could safely hold all the power – mine and theirs.

But somewhere in the last year, as my body stuttered through unpredictable cycles and a host of frightening symptoms, I'd begun to feel weak and vulnerable.

My daily stiffness and unprovoked aches made me feel like I was turning into the Tin Man in the Wizard of Oz. My legs couldn't bend like they used to. My shoulders complained every time I washed my hair. My spine grew rigid. Most worryingly, I realised my thoughts were becoming inflexible too. I felt like my choice to be any different had been taken away.

"I can't go on like this," I'd told Tay as my frustrated tears soaked the front of their T-shirt. I'd stayed the night with them and they'd thoughtfully brought me tea in bed the next morning. But my hand shook as I took the mug, tea slopped over the rim, and my tears welled instantly. Tay had taken the mug from me and placed it safely on their bedside cabinet, then gathered me in their arms, held me firmly against their chest, and gently rocked me.

"Let us help you."

I'd had to surrender. There was no other way. Tay and Bree were the two people I trusted most in the world. If I couldn't yield to them, I was doomed to end up like one of the dancing women: forever turned to stone.

My back had begun to prickle on top of the granite and I'd lodged my fingertips into the grooves. Tay held tight to my ankles as Bree started humming a tune I didn't recognise – a repetitive and hypnotic round in a low key. She swept her soft palms in slow circles over my chest, brushing my nipples and sending little electrical surges that made a direct line of connection to my cunt. Tay tugged a little on my feet, lengthening me and pivoting my hips wider.

"Good," they praised. "That's it, you're gonna have to let go sooner or later. We're gonna make you feel good. You know that, right? But first, we have to loosen you up a bit. 'Yellow' if you need to. 'Red' and we'll stop everything. You okay? You green to go?"

I took a deep breath. "Yes. Green."

Bree stopped humming and placed her hands firmly on my shoulders. She dipped her head forward and whispered in my ear, "I'm going to be right here."

Tay let go of me and stepped over to the rucksack they'd brought with them. They bent to pick out some items and when they stood, I saw they held a short flogger in each hand. The tails were made of wide, soft leather and Tay drew air circles with them as they warmed up their wrists and shoulders. Tay continued to twirl the floggers as they walked around the slab, measuring distances with their eyes, and taking in the involuntary trembles of my limbs – my body already releasing some of my stored-up tension. For a brief moment, I pictured a shaking sacrificial lamb on this slab – but my story was different; I was here willingly.

The floggers landed lightly on my chest with a one-two beat. Wump-wump.

Over and over – just enough to wake up my skin and focus my attention. Right here, right now. Tay moved further down my body and aimed at the curve of my hips. Then they increased the power behind their swings as they directed their blows to the meat of my thighs. Thud-thud. Thwack-thwack. Repetitive and concentrated strokes. Decorating me with a flushed hue that extended from my collarbones to just above my knees. In the centre of this readied space, my cunt began to throb.

My shaking was replaced by a gentle writhing; the granite felt like it was moulding to my shape – or maybe Tay was reshaping me to better fit the stone.

"Good girl." Bree's voice was beside my ear again. "Let it go, baby."

Then her hands squeezed around my breasts, causing me to take a sharp intake of breath. I exhaled with a hissing sound. "Uhuh, that's it." She gripped me tighter.

While I was distracted by Bree, Tay swapped the floggers for a pair of leather gloves. I only noticed this when they suddenly pressed a firm hand over my mouth and nose. Time froze for a moment as my breath was suspended. When they eventually moved their hand away, I gratefully gulped in a lungful of cooling, night air.

Bree moved to my feet. Tay stepped in at my side, looked into my eyes and smiled before striking me, two-handed. They delivered a solid whack with gloved palms that landed forcefully on my chest and knocked the air from me again. Bree pressed her knuckles into my soles. Tay struck me again, this time their palms curving slightly to smack the round of my breasts. Then they pressed their weight onto my hip bones, before seeking out the indentations where my pelvis met my thighs and pushing their thumbs into me. I felt myself begin to liquefy at their proximity to my cunt. I wanted more inside me.

Bree held my ankles firmly and leaned her weight back a little – stretching me longer as I felt myself simultaneously grow wider. Then she lifted my legs and pushed, forcing my knees to bend and my hips to splay. She held me in this position, my soles pressed together, my knees out to the side, my cunt completely exposed.

Tay ran their leather-clad fingertips over the sensitive flesh of my inner thighs. "Sweet and soft," they commented. "Pale and pure." They traced invisible patterns over and around my flesh, drawing ever closer to my aching cunt.

"Please," I whispered.

A hard slap landed on my right inner thigh. It stung instantly but I was quickly distracted by the same treatment to my left. Then Tay balled their hand into a fist and drew their elbow back.

They paused. "Look at me."

In the haze of the dusk light, I could see the love and care etched into the expression on their face. I could also see their lust, their hunger, and their need to hurt me in order to heal me.

"Please," I repeated.

Tay grinned, aimed, and punched directly where their slaps had previously landed. Two to the right, to the left. Then again and again, fast and furious, until we were both breathless.

My skin throbbed and burned, and I was sure bruises were already blossoming from Tay's concentrated pummelling. I drank in the sensations, feeling a deep sense of belonging in this body of mine. In recent months, all I could think about was wanting to escape from my skin, to be able to step out from the confinement of my muscles and bones and fly free. But here I was, not flying but floating on a sea of endorphins, dopamine, and the deep intimacy of connection and shared desire.

"It's time," Bree swapped places with Tay and lay one hand over my heart and the other over my mound. She waited until my breathing slowed. "We love you," she reminded me. Tay handed her a bottle of lube and she poured a generous amount over her fingers and palm. Then she dribbled more directly onto my cunt and I felt it channel down my lips, over my arsehole, and onto the surface beneath me. I felt the contrast: the soft malleability of my flesh and the steadfastness of the stone.

Stars were beginning to dot the darkening sky. I gazed up at them and remembered once being told that we are all made of stardust.

Bree slid three fingers inside me with ease then immediately retracted them and moved in with a fourth. "You are so ready for this," she reassured, slowly rotating her fingers to stretch me wider. I felt her thumb land in her palm and her knuckles nudge at my entrance. "I'm going to fuck you until you remember who you are," she told me. "It might hurt a little, but it will be a good hurt."

I felt the pressure of her hand pushing inside me, her fingers curling, my resistance relinquishing, and then... an exquisite fullness. A feeling of wholeness.

Bree moved her fist slowly. A gentle push and pull blended with the slightest rotation.

I felt something hidden deep in the core of me begin to surface, and then a sudden feeling of panic overwhelmed me. "I can't," I gasped.

Tay weighted me down with their palms on my chest, anchoring me. "Yes, you can."

"You can," Bree echoed. "This will help." Fingers from her free hand found my clit and she lightly circled it in time to her fucking. "You can," she repeated. "Say it with me."

Her hands fell into just the right rhythm. The hidden part of me began to break free. "I can," I whispered. "I can. I can. I can." Then, "I am. Bree, I'm gonna come. Tay, Bree, I'm..."

Guarded by the stone circle, protected by my lovers, I remembered how to dance.

9

Dryad by Jaymie Wagner

"I know this was my idea, but I'm still a bit nervous," Carmen admitted as she stepped out of the car.

I gave her a reassuring smile as I walked around the car, then brought her close for a gentle hug.

"If it doesn't feel right, it doesn't feel right. We can just have a nice walk in the woods and go home, no questions asked."

I felt the warmth of Carmen's breath through my top as she took a deep breath, then nodded.

"I do want this. I just...it's a lot."

I nodded again, and kissed the top of her forehead.

"I mean, it's just you and me *not* having sex in a public forest. Nothing we haven't seen before."

She snorted a laugh as she stepped out of my embrace, then lightly slapped my arm as I reached for the backpack I'd put in the back of the car.

"Sass."

I grinned as I took in her willowy figure, long red hair done into a cute braid. She'd put her favorite brown underbust corset over a soft green dress, and I could already feel myself stirring as I drank in her beauty.

"You love it and you know it."

Carmen made a point of grumbling, but the flushed cheeks and smile made it clear how she really felt as we left the parking lot and made our way down towards the woods.

"Any particular path you want to take?"

Carmen shook her head as she looked around. "Not really. Just...deeper in the forest, I think. I know there's a risk people could find us, but I want this to be...intimate."

I gave a happy little murmur. "I like the sound of that. If we take the next fork to the right, it goes up into a pretty dense wooded area."

Carmen nodded as she stepped closer, her hand running gently up the small of my back and making me shiver.

"Let's go, then."

We walked down the path, enjoying the beauty of the forest and the pleasant afternoon weather until the canopy thickened and the shadows lengthened.

I was surprised that we hadn't heard or seen anyone else in the woods aside from some distant stomping along the trails and snatches of laughter carried on the gentle breeze. There had certainly been plenty of cars and bikes around when we arrived.

I began to wonder if the forest itself was conspiring to make sure Carmen would feel comfortable, but I knew that was a bit silly. After all, it was alive, but it wasn't really *alive*, right?

After hiking for an hour, we hit a small clearing. A large oak stood at the center and flowers were scattered about the grass, adding their perfume to the moss and woodsy smells.

The breeze had fallen off as we walked into the clearing, giving it an almost hushed air – as if it had been waiting for us to arrive. Carmen walked ahead of me, then slipped her shoes off before wandering barefoot around the clearing, disappearing behind the tree for a moment.

"*Here*," she said in an almost reverent tone as she reached out to run a hand along the oak's bark. "This is the place."

I grinned, trying to mask my excitement as I took off the backpack I had grabbed from the car and pulled out a thick picnic blanket. "Where should I put this?"

Carmen took a slow turn before pointing to a spot a few feet away.

"Over there," she said as something seemed to shift in her bearing. I nodded and walked over to where she had pointed, turning my back as I shook the blanket out.

"Drop it," she ordered in a stern tone, and I let the blanket fall from my hands.

"Good girl," she purred in a husky voice that filled my brain with sparks before diving down my spine and into my crotch.

When I looked back to where she had been standing, Carmen's spine was straight, her shoulders set, her braids let out into a loose ponytail. As the sun turned her hair to flame, it was as though she had been transfigured by the power of nature.

"You've made such a mistake," she murmured as she slowly sauntered towards me. "Coming into this forest with me."

I worried at my bottom lip as I stared back at her, fixated by the sudden change of roles.

"What mistake was that...?"

Carmen's sultry laugh was intoxicating me as she came close enough to cup my face, running her thumb oh-so-slowly over my cheekbone.

"Wandering into the woods with a Dryad, you silly little thing."

My lips formed a wordless 'oh' as her hands moved to my shoulders, pushing me inexorably backwards. It didn't matter that I was a big girl with big curves and that she was maybe a hundred and fifty pounds soaking wet, lean and sleek as a ballet dancer. All my strength vanished the moment she had spoken, my resistance melting with every word.

She was the one in charge now, and I had no choice but to obey.

"These trees give me power," the Dryad murmured as she pushed me back into a thick tree trunk. "The longer we're here," she purred happily, "the stronger I become - and the weaker you will be."

The top I had chosen was thin enough that I could feel the rough edges of the bark scraping against my back, and I let out a little whimper.

"Mmm, I see you enjoy that idea. Do you like me making you a weak, helpless little girl?"

I nodded, unable to trust myself to say more. The shapewear panties I'd worn felt so tight now, and I knew my skirt had to be tenting.

As if she had read my mind, the Dryad reached down to rub at me through the fabric, and my heart stuttered as I moaned into her touch.

"What a desperately needy little thing you are," she observed as she squeezed mercilessly, pressing herself against me to pin me in place.

"It's almost like you *want* to get caught, you silly. Little. Girl."

"Yes," I gasped as I tried in vain to find a bit of leverage, a touch more friction. Squirming around to get just a bit of relief that the Dryad mercilessly denied at every turn.

"This is my forest," she whispered into my ear before moving to kiss and nibble at my neck. "You don't get to cum without my permission."

"I won't! I promise I won't!"

The Dryad scoffed as her hands pinned my arms to my sides. "You promise you won't, what, hmm?"

"I promise I won't cum without permission, Miss!"

She released one of my hands so she could take my chin and turn my head to meet her gaze, molten heat in her sky blue eyes.

"We'll see about that."

She pushed my skirt and panties down in one swift move, fabric pooling around my ankles as she mercilessly began to run her hands up and down my sides.

"You will keep your hands on my tree, or I will use its branches and vines to tie you up, you desperate slut."

I nodded as my fingers tightened against the rough bark, losing my words every time the Dryad's thumbs flicked over my nipples, shuddering with need as her thigh pressed between mine.

Mischief twinkled in her eyes as she continued to tease me with touches and kisses, never quite getting me to the edge before she backed off and started again, each touch building a fire inside of me that could only be quenched with one thing.

"P-please," I gasped as she lavished my neck with kisses and bites. "Can... can I cum, Miss?"

The Dryad's hair tie had slipped out somewhere along the way, sending her flaming hair cascading down her shoulders. Her eyes were wide with feral glee, and her hungry gaze bored into my eyes.

She had truly become a part of the forest - a wild and uncontrollable force of nature, drawing power from the life around us to keep me weak and submissive to her will.

"Will you obey me whenever you come into my forest?"

"Yes Miss!"

"Will you come to this clearing whenever I call you here?"

"Yes Miss!"

She slipped closer, moving to the side. The Dryad, reached out to take one hand from where I had somehow managed to keep it still and placed it on my aching girldick.

"Finish," She commanded in my ear. "Give yourself to My Forest!"

I barely needed the encouragement, pumping myself away as my back arched and I pressed my head back into the trunk with a cry. I felt myself throb and shake as I came, spurting out over my hand and into the grass and tree roots.

"*Yes*," the Dryad exclaimed with her own blissful moan as she reached around to pinch and fondle my breast, teasing new moans and cries from me as I continued to stroke.

Another peak of ecstasy made my knees weak, and I felt like I was close to collapsing in a heap when Carmen gently took my hand away, her voice softening.

"Shhh...good girl. You did so well my love."

I nodded as I tried to get my breath back, aftershocks still buzzing through my nerves as I sank down to my knees, the blades of grass tickling against my bare legs. I felt like I had just ran a marathon - or experienced a miracle. My brain and body needed a moment to find themselves, and I finally felt as if I could breathe again.

"Holy fuck, gorgeous!"

Carmen giggled as she gently guided me up and away from the tree and towards the blanket, kicking it out a bit more before she helped me settle down on it.

"That was amazing, Carmen. I don't think we've ever had a scene get that intense before."

She nodded as we adjusted into a comfortable cuddle, draping herself over my chest so she could press a kiss to my sweaty forehead. The breeze felt cool and refreshing as I felt the wind pick up, and I could hear songbirds again.

"Something about this spot just connected with me," she murmured before kissing my cheek. "I sunk my toes into the ground and suddenly felt like this really was 'my' Forest – at least for a little while. That the forest was giving me the power I needed."

I hummed happily as I wrapped an arm around her back, gently stroking back and forth. After such an intense, intimate moment, it felt a bit odd to just be laying half naked on the blanket while Carmen was fully clothed, but it also felt really right.

"I know this was for me," Carmen asked quietly after we had cuddled for a while, "but you felt *it* too, right?"

I squeezed her as tightly as I could in response, my lips brushing over her forehead again.

"Carmen, this was so beautiful. I have no idea what I expected, but this was something really special."

"Good," she breathed with relief, then sat up so she could get a good look at me. "Now, I could help you clean up…"

I grinned at the mischievous tone in her voice. "Or?"

"You *did* just give yourself to My Forest," Carmen said as she set her shoulders back and put a firm hand on my shoulder.

"I'm sure we could find a few more things that you can offer to it while I have you here."

10

You Were Never Mine by Lilith Young

The sun had long ago set, yet I remained on my back porch in the dark, smoking a joint, watching the stars twinkle through the trees. My mind was still whirling with the chaos of the day. I was in love with my backyard; it was always there for me and never judged me. Nothing but dark woods for miles. Everyone made fun of me for moving to the countryside, far away from the city, but nothing could beat the silence of the country.

So when I heard the gravel crunch under the wheels of a car driving up my driveway, I got pissed. The last thing I needed was someone disturbing my peaceful porch time. If my mother was about to show up to yell at me once again about how my perverted life was ruining hers, she could shove it. I was not getting up. She could search for me. A car door slammed. Then nothing for ten minutes. I was about to grab my shotgun and go see who the hell was on my property when I heard her.

"Hey, can I get a hit?" a timid voice said as I looked up in shock.

"Amy, what the fuck?" I bit out.

"Look, I'm sorry." She sat down next to me on my ragged brown couch.

"Sorry for what?" I spat. "Being a bitch? Marrying that asshole instead of me? Accosting me in a fucking parking lot this morning?"

"I... I shouldn't have come here." She stood and turned as I grabbed her wrist.

54

" Here. You can stay," I passed her the joint. I wanted to turn her away. But I couldn't bring myself to. We both knew where this was going and how it would end. Yet I couldn't stop myself.

"So what was it this time?" I teased. "He snores too loud? Wants you to quit your job? Or did he catch you with another woman?"

"We both know the only woman I have ever kissed is you," she said as she sank further into the ratty torn up couch and closer to me.

"Should I count myself lucky then?"

"I think it's me that is lucky," she whispered as she leaned closer to me. My mind began to reel, but my thoughts were clouded and high. My self control had been blown away with the wafting smoke. I turned to gaze at her as I took another hit, leaning in to meet her mouth. She opened her lips, welcoming the smoke as I blew my last bit of self preservation into her. Our tongues crashed into each other, erasing the past ten years of time and pain. I pulled her into my lap as I gripped her thighs.

"Fuck, I've missed you," she cried out as she rolled her hips into me.

"You poor little girl. Your sugar daddy not meeting all your carnal needs?" My hands traced up her chest, her full breasts falling into my hands like they were coming home. "Shit, you still don't wear a bra? Such a fucking slut."

"God, just for you... just for you," she moaned as I pinched her nipples and pulled.

"Where does he think you are?" I asked, cursing myself for being so turned on at the idea of fucking someone's wife.

"Shit, Target. He thinks... I'm at Target." Her breath was rough as I bit down on her neck. My body arched into hers as I ripped her shirt off.

"Such a sad lonely housewife, so desperate for anyone to fuck her. Look at you and your perfect fucking tits." I pulled her full breasts into my mouth as she cried out. Suckeling at the source of life, I lost myself. Tossing her to the side, I jerked down her jeans and kneeled before her. Grabbing her thighs, I yanked her to the edge of the couch and spread her legs wide. "You are perfection. Fucking Hell."

"Shit, Elle. Wait..." she called out.

"No," I sneered as I licked up her dripping wet cunt. "So wet for me. Such a desperate whore. You don't really want me to stop, do you?" I slowly swirled my tongue around her swollen clit.

"God, no. Please don't stop. I... Oh Christ. Right there..." Her moans echoed through the silent woods. I slid two fingers into her sopping wet pussy, curling them into her pleasure. Her legs wrapped around my shoulders, squeezing me as her cunt pulsed tightly around my fingers. I pulled up and bit down on her inner thigh. She cried out.

"Ow! God damn it Ellie." I bit down harder, and with each bite, she gushed all over my fingers.

"God, you like this, don't you? You are making such a mess, you nasty little whore." I sucked her juices off my fingers. "Fucking delicious." I drank down every drop and slid back in.

"Yes, yes...you feel so good. Oh shit...How do you feel so good?" she moaned out.

"Because you have been fucking a man and not me," I growled out in anger as I flipped her over and onto all fours, pounding my thick calloused fingers into her waiting cunt as she sat up and leaned against me.

"I'm sorry... I'm sorry," she whispered as tears began to fall down her cheeks. Ignoring her tears, I relentlessly fucked her as she hung onto me. Clinging to the past for a brief moment in time, as if nothing existed outside of us.

"I know love, I know," I sang to her as I slid a third finger in, pushing her over the edge. I could feel her climax pulsing around me as her body shivered against me. I slowly pulled my fingers in and out of her to prolong her pleasure, not wanting this moment to end. Our bodies wrapped around one another, orgasmic bliss passing between us with each pulsing movement. I slid out of her and fell onto the couch, pulling her into my lap.

Our energies still combined and sizzled between us as I sprinkled kisses all over her tear soaked face. The heavy silence creeped into our sacred space as the repercussions of what we just did washed over me. Sensing my body tense, she looked up at me.

"I shouldn't have come here," she said again with a tone that felt like ice water splashing onto my face.

"No, you shouldn't have," I calmly replied, refusing to play along.

"I'll just go then," she said as our eyes met, searching for something. Anything to save this, us. But there wasn't anything we could do. There was nothing she was willing to sacrifice for me. It shouldn't hurt. God though, it still did. I did the only thing I knew to do, hurt her before she could hurt me anymore than she already had.

"Go home to your husband," I whispered in her ear. "Will you you fuck him tonight? Tell him how big his cock is as he slides into you? Such a pathetic slut."

"God, you are such an asshole!" she yelled at me as she jumped out of my arms and pulled on her clothes.

"What does that make you? That has always been your problem. You think you are the victim in everything. I didn't show up at your house. I didn't beg you to fuck me. I'm not the one who is fucking married!" I screamed at her until my voice was hoarse.

"Why would anyone marry you?" she snarled. "Always alone out here stoned, you couldn't get anyone to commit to you if you tried."

"Just get the fuck out and don't come back," I said with desperation as I sat down on the porch steps and she stormed off. I held my breath as I listened to the gravel move under her tires driving away. *I will not cry. I will not cry.* I reached into my shirt pocket and pulled out another blunt.

Lighting it up, I drew the smoke into my lungs. Ready to disappear.

11

The Shower by Ryder West

I stepped gingerly out of the passenger seat of the Subaru and gently shut the door, careful to keep my arms awkwardly low. The surgical compression vest chafed at my armpits as the desert heat began its slow overwhelm of my body. At least, I thought, after I beat this final boss of binders, I will never have to experience underboob sweat again.

My fingers barely grasped the strap of my backpack before you swatted at them.

"That is definitely more than five pounds!! Wait for me, I'll grab it for you."

This wasn't our usual dynamic - you taking the lead, making the decisions, doing things for me. I was never the type of Dom to have my submissive carry and set out our playthings. I prefer to do that myself, with devastating slowness, deliberating. I like it when you rely on me for your pleasure, your pain.

But in this phase of our relationship, I am reliant on you. The cups are on a shelf too high for three weeks post-op. I haven't washed my hair by myself in weeks. You know how much my drains measured, how I respond to stillness.

I've had enough of the stillness, and now that I'm cleared for light exercise, I can't imagine sitting still.

You move our bags into the AirBnB, the blast of cool air a shocking contrast as we step over the threshold. You allow me to carry in our coffee cups and I set them on the butcher block counter before sinking into the cool leather of the couch. You set the final bag on the chair and sink next to me, thighs touching.

The closeness is electric.

"So when the sun goes down, maybe we can go into the park and hike to see the stars?" I ask. My mind is ablaze with all the things I want to do with you, alone, liberated from the requirements of keeping my heart rate low. You on your knees in the dirt, my hand gripping the base of your skull, grinding my hips into your willing tongue…

"Love! He said nothing strenuous," you interrupt my daydream as if you can hear my thoughts.

"I know I know! I just need to move. He did say I can start to work out again." I pout.

"I know, my love. You're healing. Maybe we start with a walk later tonight?"

I hate this negotiation, even though I know you're right. Your scars have faded over the last 3 years, and it comforts me to know you've been right where I am.

"I need a shower. The heat is killing me in this devil-binder. I have no idea how you grew up in this." I shift to rise from the couch without putting pressure on my arms. Gotta keep those incisions thin.

"The booking says this place has an outdoor shower…" your voice trails off. The outdoor shower: the pinnacle of all AirBnB home conversion tropes. You've always been a little bit of an exhibitionist, but somehow still shy about your desire to be seen, maybe caught.

"Well, let's go find it."

Outside the sliding glass door is a path that leads to our destination. A loose fence of wooden slats corrals the shower head, mostly obscuring us from the neighbors.

My mind is a kaleidoscope of fantasies. Possibly even some surgeon-approved ones.

"Start the water." I drop my voice a little, into that tone that makes you weak at the knees. "I'll grab towels from inside."

You let out the tiniest of moans.

"Yes, Sir."

I retrace my steps back to the house, unhooking the eyes of the hellish binder and peel off my shorts as quickly as possible. For this to work, you can't suspect a thing.

I had snuck the strap and my favorite dildo into my backpack before we left. The leather is cool to the touch against my hip bones as I fasten the straps, securing my cock into place. It's a purple piece, not too thick, perfect for fucking your throat.

I wrap a towel tightly around my waist, securing my nipple dressings with tape, and take a second to revel at my shirtless form in the mirror. My scars, still covered in tape, are rapidly becoming my favorite part of my body.

I grab another towel for you and head back outside.

Your back is turned, water streaming down to the small of your back and rolling off your ass. I could watch you for hours; the rivulets against your smooth skin, the beads at the tips of your cropped blonde hair, the way you hum lightly at the pleasure of your naked body under warm water. I remove the towel and press my body into yours, firm cock pressing between your cheeks. Your hum becomes a moan as you turn to face me.

"Be a good toy and get on your knees for me." My voice is low, quiet, once again authoritative.

You pause for a second, deliberating. "Well, you are cleared for exercise..."

You sink to your knees against the wide slats that form the shower wall, arms folding behind your back just as you've been trained. I step underneath the stream of water, lifting my cock to your lips. Your tongue willingly meets it, mouth surrounding the piece as I gently thrust my hips. The water ripples from my shoulders onto your face and you gasp for air.

I pull my dick from your mouth. "Is this alright, my love?"

You moan, nodding enthusiastically.

Alright, then.

I thrust myself back into you, slowly. The water is in stark contrast to the desert air, almost chilly until my hips rock me back into the unyielding sun. You crane your neck to take more of me and I grab your hair, enforcing the agony of patience. Inch by inch I take more of your mouth until I can feel my cock hit the back of your throat.

I freeze. "Tell me you want it," I growl.

Your feet kick against the shower floor as you moan in protest. I know you hate speaking your desires, but I both love and find reassurance in hearing you tell me how much you enjoy the brutality. I yank your head off of my cock by your hair and meet your eyes.

"Well?"

"I want you to fuck my throat, Sir," you breathe.

I groan, my unrelenting grip on your hair forcing the dildo to the back of your willing throat. I continue to press, pushing myself further into you, filling your throat with my shaft. My clit aches behind the silicone, throbbing at the sight of you on your knees for me. Your blue eyes water, fists gripping the air as you fight to stay in place. My good toy.

I relent, pulling out of your throat just as your feet start to kick, and you gasp for breath. My thumb wipes away the tears from your eyes.

"Such a good fucktoy." My voice is barely above a whisper.

You barely have time to whimper before my cock fills you again. You gag and sputter as I rock my hips into you over and over, claiming your breath, your air, your body as mine. I can feel my own wetness dripping down my thighs. Your hands grip my ass as I gag you with my dick once again. The fact that it's a struggle only makes it hotter that you fight to stay on your knees for me.

I grip your hair and pull my cock from your throat, allowing you to catch your breath. My thighs are sticky, but I'm not in the mood for using this shower for its intended purpose. I pull the dildo up toward my stomach, resting my foot on the shower bench, clit inches from your face.

"Clean it up," I command.

The words have barely escaped my mouth when your lips wrap around me. I can feel how eager you are, moaning into my cunt. Your tongue flutters against my opening before you turn your attention back to my clit, sucking as if your life depended on it. I groan, palms bracing against the wooden slats that form the walls of the shower. My hips grind into your face and I let out a low moan, which you return as my legs start to shake. My hand grips your hair, desperate for more of you.

You know just what to do - you always do. Your tongue flicks against my swollen clit. Your fingers curl inside me in that intoxicating, practiced rhythm we have built together for nearly a year. You are steady, consistent. A good fucktoy that knows exactly how to make their Sir come. I'm overwhelmed by it all - the desert sun, the now frigid water, the building ache between my legs, the newness of my body in this form.

My orgasm overwhelms me, filling your mouth with my juices, your hands with my quaking flesh. I maintain my grip on your hair - for stability, but also because I need to feel you there.

My shaking subsides, labored breaths slowing as I release you and fumble with the shower.

"That's my good fucktoy." My voice is gravelly, low. "You better not have missed a single drop."

***

Later, before bed, you kiss the back of my neck as you help me back into my surgical binder.

"Thanks for taking care of me earlier," you whisper.

Our eyes meet in the mirror and you give me a wink.

Right back at you, my love.

12

George by erin riley

I have gone to Berlin to meet George. In Berlin, I know only Gareth, my friend from university who moved here because you can have a disability and a creative life, not like in Australia where you can't pay the rent.

The first week in Berlin, I find Gareth at his sublet in Neukolln. He's moved in with a grey-haired dyke called Vonnie and gets to practice his German all the time. They make dinner for me – roast vegetables, fresh sourdough Vonnie baked and kraut. Gareth's cooked himself chops, his chronic fatigue steeled by a solid daily dose of red meat. When we finished, Gareth plonked the pan outside on a balcony colder than a fridge.

I'd brought dessert from the bio and offered the final slice of chocolate cake to Vonnie.

'No thanks'

'Are you sure?'

'Why would I say no if I wanted it!?'

I had not understood what Gareth had meant by *'very German'* when he had described Vonnie to me but I presumed this to be it.

After dinner, we go into Gareth's room and he disrobes, tossing his shirt and pants into a corner of crumpled clothes, nakedness his preferred outfit. He slumps in his Y fronts against the side of his bed on the floor. We drink fake beers and watch the rain beat against the window. I tell him about George.

The weekend before I leave for Berlin, you and I have coffee at the café under our apartment where the barista calls me George. I went in there, years ago now, for the first time – the first of many weekday mornings, my face still soft with sleep to get us coffee. He asked me my name, and I replied, simply and effortlessly, *George.*

I am trying to understand who George is. I am George, or part of me is George, and when I go away, I want to embody him more fully.

You are sick, and have been for so long. The kind of sick that is made when people hurt you before you are even old enough to tie your own shoelaces. The kind with no answers, only devastating and predictable in how it annihilates you. We don't have sex much because you are so sick. This is understandable and I enjoy jerking off to porn, it's easier than navigating people most of the time, but sometimes I have an urge to fuck other people.

We had a threesome once with your friend from work. I had never had one before and so we thought, let's take him home.

I meet you both after work at a bar, a block from our place. I arrive late and you have done some of the work already. Your colleague is standing close to you by the bar and you are lifting curls out of his eyes. I say hello to you both, order a whiskey, neat. He is handsome, with brown marble eyes and dark curls tight on his head. He takes up less space than is usual for a man. After our third drink, he has his hand on my thigh under the table as he kisses you on the mouth. We leave the bar, walk the few streets home and once inside, it is not long until we are tangled in bedsheets and each other. I suck him off while you watch with a heat in your eyes. We are exhausted by the end. He showers, says goodnight and wheels his bike down the street.

Since that time with your workmate, I have been thinking more about George. That time he was five, wearing the blue BMX tracksuit, at the bike park with his brother Simon and some friends, and he was using the boys' bathroom and they all screamed at him *'get out of here, it's not for girls!'*

I told my high school friend Jen about George when we went to the beach one sweltering afternoon. I felt like an outsider but beyond the breaking waves, those feelings evaporated into the salty air. I said to Jen I was not sure if I was a girl and I thought something was wrong with me. I told her that inside me was a boy called George.

Jen said that she could sense him, that I could be George to her if I wanted to. I called Jen on the home phone and when she picked up, I would deepen my voice and tell her it was George calling. *Hi George*, she would reply.

You say you had been waiting for me to tell you about George and you notice him in the way I hold my body, in how I ask to be touched and in what I tell you is too painful to look at. *I love you George*, you say, and there are tears. *Have a nice time in Berlin meeting George*, you say.

Less teeth remember, you add, encouragingly.

On the second week in Berlin, I fuck a minor celebrity who is on holidays trying to be noticed less.

My sublet is an airy studio in Kreuzberg up five flights of stairs. Inside, it's spacious and sparse.

A wooden desk is pressed into a corner by the window that spans the length of the room.

Outside, the top branches of trees, naked of their summer leaves, wave at me and on windy days, tap the glass as if saying hello.

Each Saturday, Dad, Simon and I would do the shopping. I pushed the trolley and jumped up on it as it sped down the aisles and dad would boom, *be careful!* For years I thought that under the hand rail of an escalator were thousands of tiny blades that would slice my fingers off because that's what dad told me once. He would say, *stop doing that and act like a girl!* whenever I did anything that Simon did with impunity.

I meet the minor celebrity by chance at a café on Reichenberger Strausse, not far from my studio. I am reading the new Deborah Levy novel which is about doppelgangers. It is about what I am doing here, in Berlin, looking for my double, George. I had started reading it in bed last night, the page lit by the soft orange hue of the replica Nesso table lamp.

Outside it's gloomy and wet, so I keep reading. I have come to Berlin to give George some time and space to know himself, but also because I'm not sure how I want to live my life anymore. I've been working as a therapist for a decade now, but almost overnight, the problems of other people felt so heavy, as if I was heaving behind me a huge sack of rocks.

When I am seven, Mum and I go shopping. I see a T-shirt that reads 'World's best big brother.' I ask Mum, brightly, if she can buy it for me. She looks down, her face ashen. She is grief-stricken and afraid and, in that moment, she is not my mother and I burn with shame. I mumble, *it doesn't matter* and though inside I wish to disappear, I skip ahead as if nothing is wrong. I do not let her see my tears.

It is this moment that I begin to forget about George. I speak about him less. He brings out a storm in Dad and Mum will not look him in the eyes. I stop asking for things that George would like and I learn the language of being a girl. I put clips in my short hair, because this is the person my parents want – and they reward me with open loving faces and sometimes even hold me close.

I lift my head from the book and the minor celebrity is smiling at me. I am perplexed by the fact that this attractive semi-famous person is looking at me with such warmth and, if it were not for the wall at my back, I'd have turned around to see who they were flirting with.

It has been a long time since I've seen eyes like that. Eyes that speak. I know what his eyes are asking and mine reply, absolutely, yes.

I pay for my coffee and place my book into the rumpled calico bag that holds inside it a black biro, a small beige coloured notebook, my phone, some crumpled euros and the keys to the studio.

I walk slowly, giving the minor celebrity time to catch up. I feel him, a heat at my back. I turn as I get close to the apartment and he's not far behind, hair golden and curly. He's wearing a neat black sweater and faded black jeans, boots good for a Berlin winter on his quick-stepping feet.

I unlock the door, place the bag on a hook and make room for the minor celebrity to get inside. I close the door behind him.

In my twenties, I find a barber who calls me 'bro' and gives me a crisp fade like Ryan Gosling. I visit Mum to drop off the tiny LED light bulbs for her reading lamp. *Why'd you go cutting your beautiful hair, it looks ghastly,* she quips, as I am contorted under her reading lamp, trying to make things easier to see.

I pull my shirt off. The minor celebrity tugs his cock through his jeans and looks at me with his talking eyes and without clumsiness, rocks from side to side prying off the boot from each foot, sliding them out of the way. Bright white tube socks on his feet. I unbutton my jeans, slowly, slip them off. I lead him to the bed. I hear your encouragement in my ears, *no teeth,* as I suck him off with attentive purpose. I ask the minor celebrity to take off his clothes and he obliges, slow enough for it not to be over too soon.

The minor celebrity climbs down next to me on top of the crisp pastel green sheets that remain free of his spoils that sit neatly in the divot-y terrain of my chest, a small river running after a long drought. He kisses me on the mouth and heat rises from my cunt to my throat. I clean up in the small bathroom and when I return to bed, the minor celebrity is devouring a croissant. On my pillow he points to another.

The minor celebrity has olive skin and cheeks dusted with freckles. There's a dent on the bridge of his nose. I peel flakes of croissant and eat them slowly. Crumbs cover my chest and the minor celebrity licks them off playfully, eyes locking mine. A smile emerges offering his face a hot goofiness.

The minor celebrity tells me he is lost. *'I am trying to find my way back to myself again.'* He spends his days painting and going to yoga class. Before Berlin, the minor celebrity had starred in a television show with global success and he'd become quite the hit. He was interviewed for magazines and gossiped about on pop culture podcasts. Fans took photos of him in the street drinking a coffee in his nice pants and posted it online. I had not seen the hit show, but remember him in a small indie film and all that comes to me is that I found him striking. I knew he was famous mainly because the internet told me so. He has a nice house in Ireland and has spent a lot of time between shooting movies fucking men in basements and hotels because the world saw him as the hooked-nose boy next door.

I clamp the minor celebrity's hand in mine. It is soft and warm. I run my thumb softly over his and I kiss his freckled knuckle. The light flits across the room. Hours pass. We sleep. We wake. I suggest, that like me, he's searching for his double too.

What's your name? he asks me.

George, I reply.

13

Claws in Me by Cosimo Vazquez

Suspended over Alice Springs, in the direction of Vietnam

I'm on a plane right now, trying to escape from my life in Melbourne. From this window, I can see the backbones of an orange desert extending until all I can see is the end of planet Earth.

This vastness reminds me of the first months when I arrived in this country from Mexico and lived in a shared house in Brunswick West. I walked into the kitchen and saw my housemate standing with a glass of water. Our relationship had been a bit rocky, and I wasn't sure where I stood with her.

"I'll tell you something about Australia, Carlos." A glimpse of satisfaction escaped from her face.

"This country is massive."

She shook the ice cubes inside her glass, as if she had just revealed a secret. As if knowing the actual size of something is worth keeping as a secret.

"Ma-ssi-ve", the way she said it carried pride and threat at the same time.

I'm escaping this massiveness, at least for a couple of days. The thought of putting a body of water—an ocean, a huge ocean—between myself and Melbourne, gives me a deep sense of peace.

Un poquito de paz.

Three months earlier, in Melbourne

I met him a few weeks ago, while I was working a night shift at a gay sauna. I was behind the bar serving drinks. His body had the kind of complexion that makes me turn around; shorter than me, thinner than me, with a certain innocence in his face.

I follow him indirectly, putting myself in positions where the mirrors of the venue would offer his reflection. If I lose him, then there are the video cameras.

He's in his locker right now, putting chapstick on his lips. When he inclines his head to the side, he seems proud of something, as if he were evaluating a choice, with no intention of disclosing what it is.

This is the type of man I go for. This is the type of man I am usually bitten by.

I looked at the clock. I was about to finish my shift, so I decided to approach a little and accidentally hit his shoulder against mine.

"Oh, sorry, I didn't see you there," I said.

His response would give me enough information and time to make up my mind, but he didn't say anything, he just stared at me, then walked away. His face was clean, expressionless, not too handsome.

OK.

I decided to stay, and switch from staff member to patron, in order to enjoy the game of flesh and intimacy. I serve myself a double vodka, I get undressed, put a red towel on and go upstairs.

¿Dónde estás?

I searched for him. I see him. I corner him. He grabs my hand and pulls me into a room. The door closes, yet, once inside, I'm unsure. This happens when I achieve some level of privacy, when I'm about to do this absolute act of intimacy with a stranger—but I keep going.

The room is uncomfortable, but we manage.

We become intimate, not intimate, intimate, not intimate, intimate, not intimate.

Sometimes, I wonder if this is the reason I drink a little; to cope with this feeling of arriving at no recognised destination.

Later on, he would send me a message on Grindr. Then he would start to appear; in my DMs, in my house, in my bedroom—his eyes opening and closing, underneath my linen sheets.

My bedroom

I like his body. I stare at him in the shower, waiting for the cold water to run hot. He's proud of something, slightly defensive. Later on, I help him clarify what he wants to feel. I do him missionary. Softly, he puts the palms of his hands over my cheeks. He stares at me and starts to cry a little.

Yeah, cry a little.

Llora un poquito.

He puts his hands around my neck, pulls me closer, holding me as hard as he can.

He lets me know.

Loneliness has left a mark on his face too. He gets pleasure by feeling the weight of my body, the lengths of these arms that trap him, in a prison of pleasure. He breathes deeply.

My lips close around his lips.

I feel pleasure when he moves softly. I tell him this. I shake when I have the shape of his torso over me. Cowboy. The amyl allows me to remain with this feeling.

Thank you.

I put my thumbs over each side of his hip bones.

I move him.

Slow.

The candle illuminates his body.

"I'm so comfy," he says, and I wish I could take everything in this world, and put it at his feet. Yet, I only have the palm of my hand, moving gently over his body. He lays on his side, looking at me.

I see him getting dressed. I stare at his feet. His fingers have a funny shape, they have a larger than usual space in between them, they are short. "Ugly," I think to myself, and smile.

I liked that he was imperfect. That was the moment, I think I fell in love.

Casi al final

Life will treat me the way it does before it releases me.

It will close doors, one by one. Slowly, leaving me without air.

And just when I think I'm doomed, a flower in my heart will blossom.

This is how it ends.

He's gone.

I just started my shift, it's 2:00 AM, and the venue is busy. "Can I have two towels," I hear him ask at the bar, I stare at him and it takes a few seconds to re-connect the memories. By now, I had forgotten his voice, that raspy voice that seemed to come from a cave, as if his true self was trapped down underneath and I could only hear the echo.

I see his face, yet I'm surprised how my body is able to block any emotion and keep a straight face, and look away. Two towels. One for him, and one for the other latino standing behind him.

A kind gesture.

I see him — I see them. The story repeats, but this time I'm watching a movie scene unfolding without me. I have no part in it. There he goes again, to care deeply for him. They exchange numbers in front of me, they say goodbye with a kiss.

I smile at the thought that he's fucking the gay Latino community, one at a time. I finally have the courage to block him everywhere.

He's gone and I'm free, wondering what to do with this freedom.

14

Offer Up by Jordan Asher

"I want to offer something if you like, something for you to think about. Tell me what you're secretly wanting . . . You could just try it."

With his words in mind, I deeply considered what my body wanted, maybe even, what it needed.

My partner Theo, dropped me off at the airport with the biggest smile, they knew this is what I've longed for. As the wheels lifted off the runway, I grabbed my notebook to write. The sense of existential dread hits me and brings me to the page in the best ways at a cruising altitude of 31,000 feet. It was different this time though. This time, I sat in discomfort.

While my carefully curated queer playlist buzzed in my ears, I sifted through my messages. I was finally meeting *you* and for the entirety of the flight I couldn't sit still. I kept reading Theo's affirming last text message, telling me how proud they were. Leaning into the uncomfortable freedom of untapped desire is not an easy feat.

But just as planned and predetermined, I'm finding my way.

I checked into my hotel and got ready. Nervously staring at myself in the mirror, I kept feeling like my much younger self, anxiously awaiting a field trip and unable to sleep through the night. I wore my favorite lingerie set under my vintage black jeans.

I unbuttoned and pushed my jeans down and sat on the long bathroom counter. I found the angle I needed and knew so well and sent a picture to Theo. Giving into the rush of finally meeting you, I slid off the cold sink counter.

I added a subtle gray corset top paired with a corduroy jacket and finally messaged you that I was on my way.

My body felt so warm from the Uber ride to your hotel, the heat building in my chest with each mile that passed.

I was determined to embrace any awkward silence by reminding myself that the newness is always the fun part. The longing and yearning is so fucking good. I saw you at your hotel bar just like we planned. I couldn't miss the uniform I knew you wore so well and the black tourmaline around your neck that you adored for more than just a good omen.

I nudged the butterflies I could feel over and over again because I knew they weren't going away. You hugged me so tight and my body melted like it knew what to do. You had a drink for me ready. Sweet, sour, and neat. It was barely noon, but I didn't mind taking the edge off.

We started with small talk and you placed your hand on my thigh. I lit up, grateful for the comfort. Small talk turned into a meaningful exchange just as I thought it would. I wanted to lose track of the time and make everything stand still, to soak it all in.

My phone lit up and caught my eye. I couldn't believe how much time had passed by so effortlessly. Theo had responded to the picture from earlier. In return, they sent me a picture of them touching themself and a short message "to focus on my date," which made me blush.

You watched my reaction, and as I refocused back to you, I saw how determined you appeared, just for a second, for my attention to remain on you. Surely aware you would never have to try very hard. The balance of soft and strong tenderness was real and enrapturing.

My mind and body reverted back to my first queer crush. I gathered up the courage to playfully touch your hands and couldn't stop tracing your tattooed forearms. The rosary that encircled your right forearm, I always found contradicting yet philosophical, and it drew me in.

You asked if you could show me something you had come across in this new city. I nodded eagerly without hesitation. I closed out our tab and we stood.

You put your hands around my waist, a few fingers through just one of the belt loops on my jeans, and I felt you pull me against you. The rosary I knew so well turned into a snake. One hard tug with your right hand. Without thought, I let out the softest gasp at the feel of your packer against me.

I managed to whisper "Yes, please, Sir," into your ear. You politely thanked the bar hand as you took my card for me, pushing it into the front pocket of my jeans. Loving my reaction to your every touch, you took me by the hand.

You led me block by block as though you had navigated this city before. I was impressed with the sense of ownership and taking what's yours. The day was breezy yet the sun's presence was demanding. I saw its warmth dance on your skin and on your soft shirt, and it made me smile. We took the final right hand turn onto a narrow side street leading me through a worn gate and into a vast community garden space.

The foliage was so thick, yet obviously nurtured with care. You told me to explore, so I took you by the hand. Each individual plot was sectioned and adorned with a unique flare. Row after row they all blurred together, while lines of bloomed flowers scattered around us.

We walked for some time in mutual silence until I found a shaded bench. Quaint, candid, yet on display. Knowing this was exactly what you were looking for.

You leaned in to kiss me so tenderly with intent. Your hand back in the same belt loop as before and mine nervously playing around your waist. My mind raced at the prospect of you using your belt on me later. You felt the want in my body and placed your other hand on my hip and just one finger on the skin under my shirt. I let out an almost inaudible moan.

"Louder," you whispered in my ear.

I looked around us, expecting to see a passerby, knowing I wanted you anyway. I kissed you harder and decided to let my guard down, softly. I moved my hands from your Carhartt jeans to your neck. "Be good," you instructed, but I didn't listen, knowing that if I misbehaved you would tie me up later on.

I couldn't wait any longer and moved my hand to your zipper. I felt your packer again and moaned louder this time. You grabbed both of my hands tightly with care and led me to the bench. You sat down without hesitation.

With total bravery, I kneeled in front of you.

You unzipped your jeans and I positioned myself between your knees. As I looked up at you, I knew I needed you in my mouth.

With my hand at the base of your packer, I wanted the perfect pressure to hit your boyclit just right. All I could think about was you stroking yourself as a reward for me later that night. The light of the city washing over you while you take in your fresh bruises upon my body.

"That's enough." You gently grabbed my face. As though you could read my mind, you asked me to take the phone from the left pocket of your jeans. You took a picture of me still between your legs, looking up, wanting more.

I smiled and looked around us. "Let people see," you demanded, slipping two fingers into my mouth while simultaneously recording a video.

"Something for me to enjoy later," you smirked.

I knew then, you needed your way with me.

With one hand, you pulled me up on top of you. I heard distant conversation and laughter almost like heat encircling me. You told me to be good and unbutton my jeans. I watched you take in every second, finally getting to see my soft stomach and thighs. I fought the urge to look over my shoulder.

You took your wet fingers and teased my cunt. Learning exactly what I liked best.

It didn't take long for me to start grinding into your hand while you purposely avoided my clit to drive me crazy. Begging you with every cell in my body for what I needed, I kept whispering in your ear "Please Daddy, fuck me?" You told me to be patient, you knew what I really wanted. I kept begging you and moaned even louder. We both heard more voices. I just got louder for you. "Good girl," you reinforced.

You stopped teasing me to grab my ass. You slid me even closer to you and started slapping it harder and harder just like we talked about. You saw the pleasure and the calmness flush over my demeanor. You all but praised me every time I got louder for you.

I whispered that I needed something more, right here.

And you already knew what that would be. I watched you pull a zip tie out of your back pocket. Your hands grasped mine and I let out a small nervous laugh. You pulled me closer. I heard one of my favorite sounds as the zip tie started to bring my wrists together in front of me. "Tighter," I begged as I watched you quickly calculate, securing me to the bench behind you.

You didn't let me say anything else as you shoved two fingers deep inside me. I saw my favorite look of absolute need in your eyes, then I kissed you. My teeth accidentally grazed your top lip more than I estimated. You loved these little moments.

"Let me really hear you," you urged. I instantly felt a different warmth flush over me as you shoved another finger deep inside and I moaned so loudly.

You were so proud of the space I was claiming as ours. You felt my cunt tense around your fingers a few times and then took your fingers out of me slowly, yet without hesitation.

"Please, Daddy, please," I kept loudly pleading as I glanced to the side of me at the grooves taking form in my wrists.

Touching yourself, you whispered into my ear, "Those bruises are turning my favorite color."

I watched as you finally felt how wet you were for me. I pleaded with you to let me touch you, just like you taught me.

I started biting your neck as I felt your hips grind into mine. I kept pulling at my wrists as if I would finally be able to free just one. You heard the bench creak as I kept pulling and this drove you over the edge. I felt your body melt against mine as you came on me.

You kissed me and I watched you let me in, for one brief moment.

I felt my eyes become hot as the kiss became harder. You started teasing my clit again, bringing me fully back to you whilst tormenting me with every detail you had planned for us. I told you I couldn't wait any longer.

"Not yet," you told me over and over.

When you were ready, you told me to come. My body tensed. I let go for you and watched the look of more than just lust flicker across your face.

I knew then, that this is what my body wanted. This, is what I needed. What I was chasing started to set me free.

15

The Den by Tiger Salmon

"I found out that total creativity involves a certain intellectual rebellion – not to become a criminal, but somehow, to be totally creating, you have to do things that are a little bit forbidden."

Philippe Petit, whose wire walk between the Twin Towers in 1974 was called 'the artistic crime of the century.'

A moustached cigarette girl saunters towards me, hands me a candy cigar. Her smile gives me the boost I need to plunge onto the dance floor. I spin slowly to take in the scene, and flex my thighs into the beat. One look from side to side tells me I am outnumbered gender-wise. Almost everyone here is taller than me. I wonder if it is okay to be here? I look androgynous but am not presenting as masc tonight. People raised as boys are given license to let the earth take their weight, they have less concern about being too heavy, too hefty. I envy their capacity to take up space, and try to emulate it. Years of gender training begins to drop away as I lean into my masculinity.

Dancing helps a lot with dissociation. I flex my shoulders and twist my hips to feel into the strength of my thighs. Loosen my neck, relax my jaw. My face drops into a scowl as I let the mask dissolve, releasing my body to do its thing. My breasts flatten, my brow thickens. Any need to be pretty enough, to please, falls away. My knuckles clench and my forearms flex. I imagine my balls dropping, nestling a softly bouncing cock, their fur tickles my groin. A jaunty sidestep enters my dance move repertoire.

Gay men are so adept at grooming. Bushy sideburns emphasise square jawlines. Hair is coiffed and pecs pumped. The phallus is openly worshipped in this shrine to masculinity. Their honesty about this particular kink generates a focused hyper-masc vibe that is refreshingly calm. I start to relax. This place has been a gay male venue for decades. It is a relic to hedonism and queer culture. Lined in raw timber, the pheromones are strong. The animal has not been bleached away.

Polished black leather pants soak up the flashing lights, and harness buckles glint. A few fluttering feather boas brighten up the scene. There is a nice blend of campness and hardcore, bears and denim. I spot a litter of playful pups eager for attention. Men here are enjoying their bodies, their space. Fluid dance moves bely their muscled macho regalia. The euphoria that surfaces when we explore authentic desire is visible to the watchful eye. I spot two or three dykes, but steer clear of them for now. I'm dancing in a den of bears who brandish brotherly smiles of welcome, stepping back to make space for me. Gentle men.

A section of the club is accessible only by weaving through the crowded dance floor to a series of private alcoves defined by heavy timber partitions. I notice a few men cruise each other and disappear into them. I wish women were bold enough to entice each other into these forbidden zones. I've been watching gay men do this for years, taking mental notes.

The only emotion displayed by them is lust. A macho/camp batting of the eyelashes. Slight raising of the chin to indicate a yes. The moves are subtle, synchronous, and sensual. It takes time to build an erotic vibe. Arousal is generated, consent constructed.

Do you want me? Do you dig this?
Hunger. Lips purse. Then a sneer.
Stay with me.
Look away then lower your eyes.
Wait.
Feel the burn of their gaze and look up, there they are.
Follow me.

A dude catches my eye. His hand crosses his groin. He rubs his nipples with the heel of his palm. Then he hooks his thumbs into the harness that binds his chest. I clock that he might be trans. He holds my attention. Every other body in the room becomes a prop in our tango. Eyes lock, the cruising begins.

He edges his way towards me. His shimmy is subtle. I collect myself, pull my energy closer to my skin then turn away with a flick of my skirt. I imagine shooting a lasso over his way. It loops around his shoulders. I tug and pull tight and when I turn around he is right there in front of me, grinning. I raise my arms and twist my torso. It's getting hot in here. His hands are close. He places them on my hips. He holds me firm but allows me to move freely as we find our groove.

Already dripping, I am surprised at how fast I surrendered to his heat. It's been a while. It's his eyes, they penetrate. I can tell he will be an attentive lover, it's all in the eyes.

Desire has made me brave. I turn and lead him across the floor into a vacant alcove. It's dark. A bowl containing condoms, lube, and gloves is illuminated by a purple glow. It smells of amyl and cum, sweat, stale and fresh. I lean against the partition, one leg up on a ledge. He nuzzles my neck, and runs his hands up my thighs, under my skirt to grip my arse. I reach for his shoulders. Flexed biceps turn me on every time. My breath comes in deep and fast. I imagine him pumping and extend my neck to meet his nuzzle.
Yes.

I grab a chunk of crotch and pull him towards me. He lunges onto my thigh.
Pussy boy is hungry? I ask.
His hips lean into the rub. He grinds into me and grabs my waist.
You hungry too?
You first.

I unbutton his 501s, stud by stud, and thrust my hand into his pants. His fur is thick and I can smell his musky cunt. My fingers graze a clit dick and guttural moans emanate from deep within his throat.
Sensitive.
I meet the heat and circle it with my thumb and forefinger, gently stroking it to life, then curl my fingers, scraping his vulva hard as I prepare to enter. He sucks me inside. Our mouths slurp in response and we kiss deeply, biting lips.
Pussy boy likes a good pummeling?
I hold still until he groans and pushes himself onto my hand. He reaches for my tits, nudges my nipples with his thumbs. His cunt swallows my fingers, thrusting onto them in long slow strokes as if it is he who is entering me with a tasty lean cock. I curl my fingers up towards me to stroke his G-spot, adding a digit, and another. I flex my shoulders to bolster myself and lock my elbow into my hip, holding firm as he rides me home.

My focus is on his pleasure, filling his pussy with my lust. I watch his face, we lock eyes. He rocks my world and then he shudders. His cunt grips my hand in an undulating pulse. His guttural *oof* sound is muffled by my neck. I sigh, the first orgasm is a warm-up. He is wide open now, ready for a good fisting.

But first, my turn. I want to cum too.

I place my hand on his head, ever so gently, and push him down. He drops to his knees and lifts my skirt. My knickers are saturated. He slides them to one side and dives in. I am just about to close my eyes to savour the moment when I see a glint of silver through the wall behind him. There is a wide gap in the partition that must have been concealed by his body when we entered the booth. A whole section of the wall is missing. In my lust, I hadn't registered it at all. A leather man reveals himself, cap pulled low over his eyes. He faces me. Has he been watching us? This turns me on more than you can possibly understand. There is nothing I like more than an appreciative audience. He looks up and smiles slightly. I nod a curt hello. In front of him, kneels a long-haired lad whose head bobs in time to the beat of the dance floor only metres away. I sense the crowd of sweaty bodies, the heat, and the heave of the dancefloor just outside our booth.

My lovely new lover is also on his knees before me, sucking me off, nuzzling my cunt with the urgency of a hungry pup. I look up at the leatherman. It is like I am looking in a mirror at my sex twin. Perhaps he is thinking the same thing. He runs a hand through his lover's hair and I do the same. He rubs his other hand over his chest, rips open his shirt, and twists a nipple. I do the same. He is chuckling now.

He flexes his thighs and pulls back. I get a glimpse of his long cock, slick with saliva. He cups the lad's cheek with a tenderness that contrasts beautifully with his leather daddy machismo. As I watch I feel my cock lengthen. My boy runs his tongue along the base, and takes it deep into his mouth. He is hungry for it. I hold still and let him set the pace. The leather man is on the verge of coming, I sense the tension and wonder how long he can ride the rough and the smooth of it.

My boy looks up, *Are you okay?*
  Yes, yes, Honey. Don't stop! I am laughing now.

He pushes a thumb inside me and that's all it takes to send me over the edge. I throw my head back and a deep laugh pulses through my torso. My hips rock into his face and my knees buckle. He catches me in strong arms, an act of chivalry that sends me into a swoon. I lay open and fuckable and ready for more. I'm flying.

What's your name? I am returning to my body, the pulse of the dance beat loud in my ears.

Will.

Will?

That's my name.

Oh right. Thanks, Will. I try to collect myself. Happy I came. Getting ready to go.

But Will has other ideas. He pushes me back against the wall.

We're just getting started.

Oh.

He pulls a dildo out of the satchel tied to his back. He came prepared. Handy. I like them handy.

16

Opal by Orlando Silver

The girl twisted in my bed, all loose limbs. She talked too much. I slipped the cord around her wrists and made her still.

I knew you were one of them kinky ones, she said. I love it.

Oh yeah? I breathed, making quick knots.

I thought about the bar I had picked her up from. Her glittery boots. The way she had put her hand on my thigh, then moved it up.

I wouldn't see her again.

I had been driving through the city the night before. Outside a club there was a long line of people covered in shiny black leather. They stood huddled by a doorway. The sign on the wall was dark neon.

They were part of something, and they liked it. I was part of nothing, and I liked it more.

What's that scar, said the girl. On your shoulder, there. Is it teeth marks?

It's nothing, I said. You wouldn't understand.

Winter, last year.

My father was long dead. I had taken his ashes to that seaside place he loved. Standing on a high cliff above the ocean I threw the dark charcoal fragments of his bones into the sky.

He once told me his mother took him there, on holidays. He loved his mother. I wanted to release his atoms into air that he had already breathed.

A child watched me empty the canister into the wind.

He's dead, I said to him.

The boy shrugged as if to say, Okay. Now what?

I drove straight to my father's old shack. I had never been, but I knew the way. As I drove, my old truck groaned, shifting gears with a dense grinding noise.

I wanted the long winter. I hoped my truck would survive it.

When I arrived, I saw the old timber frame leaning, the tin roof tilting slightly. It creaked in the high wind. It too, was a dying thing.

As the sun moved across the sky I repaired the rifts in the walls, built up the bed frame so it didn't shift. From my truck I carried small pots, my favourite knife, old blankets.

I slowed down. My blood beat in my ears.

The first time was the gentlest.

The sun had just gone. I had edged myself out the door towards the woodpile, the big axe waiting.

I wonder now, should I have swung it? It would have been over faster.

It came to me in the shape of a man. I saw the eyes first, opal blue, and fell backwards a little.

It was dark, but the full moon shone. It was the man I had loved, three years ago.

I said his name out loud, like I might hold him to it. He smiled and my heart ached in that familiar way. I missed the way his hands felt, curved into my hips. I missed the way his mouth felt when he bit my body, pulling my hair back. I missed the way he had tied me to his bed frame, willingly.

It was him, but not him. It was something else.

You've been gone, I said.

He laughed, a low moan. Still, I looked him in the eye.

I live here now, he said. This is my home.

You cannot judge me. The darkness asks so much. And I was lonely, to my bones. He opened his mouth and I saw too many teeth, his smile too wide.

Something in me rattled loose. But I wanted it, my god I wanted it.

You cannot know what it is to have nothing. When something comes, then you want it all.

You cannot judge me for saying yes.

After that, at night when the moon began to climb, I would go to him.

His tongue always found my throat. He bruised my thighs with heavy hands. He lay me on the ground and hunched over me. I let go into dirt.

One night, he took me to the water. The jetty was a long sword. I walked naked to the end and when I turned he pushed me.

I saw his disfigured shoulders, bent over, as he did it. All my clothes lay like patchwork on the earth, far behind.

The lake bit at me, the cold alarming.

I cried and flailed. My tears merging with water. My body so cold it felt hot.

When his rough hands reached in, I clung to him. He covered me with his body as he lay me down. The animal warmth of him, the beginnings of soft fur showing. I felt his heartbeat pounding clear into my body. He snuffled quietly against me.

My breathing quietened. I was held.

When I felt him hard against me, I shifted my body, allowed my hips to open.

He moved into me. The pain was swift and overwhelming. It devastated.

I heard a distant sound, like an animal howling. I realised it was my own mouth. I let go into noise, the wail tearing from my body, every sorrow I ever had echoing free.

Please, I said to the creature. Please. I need it. Please.

Once it came to me as a woman. Her hair was tangled and held a thousand little treasures. Little shells from god knows where, and twigs. Eggshells from tiny birds.

Her eyes were too large, but the opal blue was there. She lay on her back under the old oak, branches twisted high.

When I knelt to lap at her cunt, it was sweet honey. It was nectar.

I worked my fingers into her. Her body was slick with need. The dark held us both, like cupped hands, and I murmured all the things that nobody had ever said to me.

She threw her head back. Raked my back with long nails.

I rubbed my body against hers and felt the swell of her breasts, tight nipples aching. I saw the arc of her neck. The noise she made was unearthly, wild. I wanted to be haunted by her.

She was looking up at the stars. They were looking back at her and then she kissed me. Her teeth were sharp points. My lower lip bled, and she licked it clean with even strokes.

She pushed me back against the oak, and knelt to me, moved her mouth down my stomach. I trembled in fear but knew better than to move.

I steadied my breath.

I held onto the tree behind me. The rough bark. The network of underground roots that formed a net that held me.

Her long tongue moved with purpose. Her breath hot, her teeth bared. The slow ascension. My absolute surrender.

I tried to anchor my body but the feeling thrilled inside my body and I jerked.

She snarled into me. I knew her teeth had nicked my soft flesh and I felt her start to tremble.

Her hunger overwhelmed her. Her muscles forced themselves into restraint, digging into earth. She knelt back and I saw the glisten of me around her lips.

The blood, the wetness of me, intermingled in the dark.

With a swift movement she pierced my shoulder with one long nail. It went clear through into the oak and the shock opened my mouth wide.

She gripped my body. Put her mouth to the wound.

I felt my body shudder again to orgasm in a helpless, terrible way.

Each night I thought, I won't go back.

But then, there was a pull in me, like a soft fishhook, slipping into my ribcage. It hurt. I wanted the feeling to stop. I clawed at my own flesh, trying to find where it hid. I pushed it down, my heart hammering.

I wanted to go. I wanted to run straight into the night, screaming, to find it.

Outside my tiny winter cabin I could hear the creature. Moving. The drag of something heavy. I knew the indent it would leave in the ground. Tomorrow I would find my doorway lined with dark scratches. Heavy footprints in the wet, winter leaves. The scent of blood drying on the old pine.

It was descending, each night, into something worse.

Two months had passed since my arrival. The moon almost gone. Just a quick scythe of silver, slicing the sky. No stars. In a few days the snow would come. The silence would come with that.

I wondered, Would it still find me? In the warped quiet that a dark winter brings?

Panic. My hands shook.

I stood by the little stove, brightly lit. The old bed with the mattress that sinks. The stack of yellow paperbacks with well worn pages. I stretched my hands out towards the light, as if it could save me.

It could always get in. If I wanted it to.

And I wanted it to.

The next night the horror was worse. Things had shifted by then, and I knew the world could not go back. I heard the rough crack of the pine trees as they fell, pushed as if by great force. The anger of the beast as it leaned against my walls. The yearning as it lay sprawled by the woodpile, calling to me with a wordless keening.

I had shuttered the windows, pulled the heavy bar across the door inside.

What had my father done, to keep it from coming in?

I sat by the fire all night, the axe on my lap. Waiting.

Love me, I wanted to say. Love me.

But there is never a good answer to that, when that is the only question.

When the next day came, I set the blaze myself. I tore up the paperbacks. I shoved everything I could into a pile. The bedsheets, the clothing. I used what was left of the woodpile to make the fire even bigger. When the flames hit the ceiling, the roof beams caught, and that was it.

I leaned on the old truck as the whole thing tilted, lurched, fell. There was a wide circle around the cabin, with the snow beginning to fall. It was over fast.

Ash fell in my hair. The deep wound in my shoulder seeped blood into my shirt.

I was done with the anguish of crying. There was nothing left.

I turned the key in the ignition and listened as the engine growled, ready.

Now. The city around me is a haze of lights, the moon a distant shape.

The girl sleeps, free of the rope I had used. Her glittery boots lie on my floor. I can see the tattoo of a star behind her ear, like a secret. I imagine the little nip of pain it must have made against her skin. I smell the salt of her sweat.

I stand and move to the window. The muscles in my arms work as I shove it open, the summer heat escaping.

There was time, there was time. I told myself.

Next Winter, maybe.

I could always go back.

17

Steady at the Wheel by SoftBoss

I'm driving my 1991 manual Toyota Corolla. The muffler groans and breathes hard. Its metal cylinder rattles against the car's body. Edges lined with rust. Razor thin blades scratch the glass. The clutch slides in and out.

I sent you a text.
 Time.
 Place.
 Clothing.

I see you on the corner. A boy standing alone. You're perfect to me. Beautiful.
 My chest cracks open. I allow myself to really feel it. I choke on the intensity of this desire. This rare connection unleashes a deep yearning within me. I watch you, completely overwhelmed in wonderment that you exist at all, and that you're mine.

I contemplate how I will break you slowly. I feel a tender violence rise up in me as I pull up beside you. I feel a pulse in my crotch. The edges of my cock are outlined in my tight blue jeans. My freshly conditioned black leather motorcycle boots shine. I leave the engine running and roll the window down.

"Get in."

I drive for hours in silence. Without taking my eyes from you, I pull off the highway. It's all dirt roads and thick bushland. The city lights disappear behind us. It's quiet but for the birds and the soft wind. It's dark but for the dying light of the sunset.

"Get out."

You're wearing stained, tight blue shorts and a filthy white singlet. You've thick, scruffy, curly hair and stocky, hairy legs. As directed, you wear starched, white, thick work socks and weathered blundstones.

I unlock the door, get out, and step towards you in one quick movement. You stumble backwards and land hard in the mud.

I stand over you.
"Look at me."
You lift your chin and look up.
"Open your mouth."

Your eyes open first. They're bright in the darkness. You open your mouth wide. I spit slowly. The saliva is thick. Hanging mid-air and painfully inching it's way down. The wetness touches your lips and you groan softly. You take it all. Savouring it.

I squat above you and I grab your jaw hard. I lean down so we're face to face. I know you feel an unbearable intensity when I'm this close to you. Parts of you want to run and hide. Avoid this all-consuming fear at all costs. The risk of authentic vulnerability, connection and being witnessed for your true self, is completely terrifying.

The hot heat of my breath can be felt inside your mouth as I whisper,
"Tell me what you want."
Your voice is small and quiet. It breaks mid word as the edges of your eyes moisten. Your voice cracks.

"I want you to… "

But the words run out, as tears fall silently down the side of your face. I gently touch your cheek, wiping them away. I suck the tears from my fingers. Drinking your fear and pain. After a breath, I slap you hard across the face. The pain is sharp and fast. The deep sting of skin on skin violence is undeniable. Your eyes are begging. I slap you again. Your cheek reddens. The heat builds. You refocus and breathe.

I'm straddling you now. My thick thighs pin you down. My cock sits perfectly on your hungry wet cunt. I slowly pull out my switchblade and your eyes widen. I rip your singlet open, exposing your flesh. I bring the knife to your chest. Pressing down until I draw blood. You're gritting your teeth as I pull the sharp edge down your skin. Beads of dark crimson pool and drip down your ribcage. You're in pain and the cold wind stings the open wound. You're determined. Wanting to prove this boy can take it. Aching to be worthy. Needing my praise.
I finger the cut flesh and draw the blood to your chin. I smother your lips in it. I slowly push my finger deep inside your wet mouth. I finger your tongue as you suck hard with your eyes closed. It's now that I see you begin to sink slowly into submission.

I adore how you're such a deep freak filled with dark depraved desire. Craving to submit. To be broken. Yearning to surrender everything and then be held in a tight, tender embrace.

"Tell me what you want."

I pull my bloody finger from your greedy mouth. You're scared but determined as you struggle to find your words. You know it's not about the answers, but rather the shame that lives deep in your gut. To be forced to honestly name your desires, needs, fantasies and fears out loud. To have to beg, plead and endure the possibility of rejection, judgement and failure. The risk feels too great. Raw vulnerability is an ocean in which you might drown.

You're almost frantic now and wild eyed. Craving. Aching for permission and release. I press my hard cock into your wet cunt as I precisely push the blade against your throat. A tumble of pressured speech pours out in response.

"I want pain. To hurt. Bleed. Be naked, exposed, on my knees. To be a good boy. For you. Make you proud... Rough. I wanna beg, plead. I want you to fuck me hard... and hold me closer."

I smile. I desire the power that comes from knowing what gets you off. What you crave alone in the dark. The power is mine to decide when, where, how and even if, I will give you anything you hunger for. The power is mine and you gave it willingly.

This is when I slide the clutch in and take it up a gear.

I stand up, lean down and grab you by your thick curly hair.

"Ok. Get up," my voice is stern and steady.

You're on all fours and try to stand. I kick you back into the mud. You're filthy now. Covered in it.

"C'mon. Get up."

You stand and I shove you in the chest with all my weight. You stumble back falling again. An edge of humiliation pierces the air.

"C'mon boy. Get up"

You scramble to your feet. There's a defiant edge in your eyes. I punch you in the chest and you fall back onto the Corollas bonnet. I punch you again and again, until I'm standing an inch from your face. I grip your cunt and feel how wet and desperate you are.

"Fuck," you gasp in response.

"Take these off," I say, gently pulling on your shorts.

You're naked now, but for socks and blundstones. It's cold out. I grip your jaw and push you to your knees where you belong. You look up at me with devotion. I live for this intimate moment.

I unzip my jeans. You wait eagerly with lip biting restraint. I know how desperately you crave this. I bring the tip to your lips. I grab your hair tight and hold you there. I see your body writhe and hear your soft pleading groans.

"Please," you beg, looking up at me. I rub my cock across your lips.

I grip the back of your head, pushing your mouth down the shaft until you gag. I hold you there as I fuck your sweet mouth. I hear you struggle. I let go. You cough up spit, gasp for air, and then smile. I stroke your hair and you look up at me as you hold my cock and begin to suck, lick and consume it. Your eyes close as you surrender to sensation.

I pull myself from your mouth and force you face down on the bonnet. The dewy metal is cold on your bare skin. I kick your legs apart and push my dick up against your soft ass as I whisper.
    "What are you?"
    "A dirty trans faggot."
    "And what do you want more than anything?"
    "For you to fuck me hard..... Please?"

I kiss your neck so deeply you cry out. I suck on your flesh until you bruise. I bite you hard so I can leave my mark. I know later you'll proudly trace your body searching for remnants of me. Conjuring me from memory when you're alone.

I take your ass cheeks, spreading them wide. I spit inside you and you fucking melt. Your legs go weak. I take my finger and trace your cunts edge. My other hand is keeping you steady. You're moaning loudly though I've barely touched you. I grab my cock and tease your wetness. You desperately push your ass out and try to slide me inside. I'm fiercely staunch. A strong embodied presence. I'm the anchor that holds you, so I can take you to the edge.
    You're moaning, swearing, begging and pleading. You're at the edge of tears, as your breathing gets heavier.

"Tell me what to do. Tell me. I'll do anything. Please, fuck me daddy. Please..Please?"

You are begging desperately.

Denial is where you always break.

And in uttering these words you can transcend shame.

Your cunt's so wet I don't need lube. On the last tearful *please* I thrust myself inside. Your body convulses, trembles and explodes. There is an eruption of swearing, moaning and gratitude. I start to fuck you. Your body begins thrusting back, pushing harder and harder. I fuck you faster as your body slams against the car and I feel you open up. I grab your waist and shoulder. Pushing my cock deeper. Pulling you back towards me with each thrust. Your tears are now abundant. Tears of pride, pleasure and relief.

You're sweaty and filthy. Aching to cum. Your cunt tries to swallow me up as I hold you closer. I feel you tighten around me. Like the tightness of when I fist you and I'm completely locked in at the wrist, consumed until you release me and we become extensions of one another.

I grip your hair and pull your head back sharply so I can see your face.

"Remember, you need permission."

You almost yell, " *I'm gonna cum!"*

Then looking directly into my eyes, *"Please, can I cum?"*

My pelvis pushes against you. You feel my full force. I hear you and don't respond.

Not yet.

"Fuck. Please? I need it."

I'm overwhelmed by the power your presence has over me. An inner conflict rages within. My strength manifests from complex vulnerability. Confronting deep wounds and fears is how I find my power. Breaking myself open is the only way I can break you.

"You can cum."

I let the words drip.

You explode in seconds. You tighten one last time as your whole body trembles. I make sure I can see your face as you let go. Mouth agape. Eyes rolled back. Head dropped. Body collapsed. You're utterly spent. Used up. Delirious. I soak it all in. I need, want and deeply desire this.

I pull out. My cock's covered in a thick slick of your cum. I scoop it from your hole as your knees buckle from my touch. I push two fingers inside your mouth. Your eyes are closed in concentration as I lift you onto the bonnet. You instinctively wrap your legs around me tightly and I grip you with an intensity others rarely see. I cradle your face in my two hands and hold you tenderly. I stroke your face and run my fingers through your thick hair.

As I stroke your cheek I tell you softly how deeply proud I am. That you're such a good boy. That you did so well. That you are mine. My boy. That I've got you.

You look at me. In this rare moment you are completely open, raw and honest. I see you. I know you And in this small moment I savour that deep but fleeting connection that I cannot find anywhere else.

You smile gently as you say, "*Thank you Daddy,*" and stroke your hand across my cheek. My heart feels devastatingly full.

In this moment under the stars, you're calm, present and free. Away from the world it's only this land and us.

In the unspoken undercurrents of taboo working class faggotry, I always found desire. I took it and ran with it. Dragging it violently through the mud. Making it defiant, filthy, deeply and perversely queer. Making it mine. In seeking the intensity of experience, I could transcend my own darkness, shame and pain, and I found others on their knees waiting for me, craving the same.

In this place of dirty submissive working class trans faggots.

I found you.

And more importantly, I found myself.

18

Biker Butches by Leo Wilder

"Such a good fucktoy. Taking your punishment so well for Sir," Jack praises. Charlie's blindfolded, tied to a tree, ass red and beaten, holes filled with toys for Jack's amusement.

A silver fox butch with long hair and an older stud are on their knees in the dirt between Charlie's legs, mouths trailing over her clit and the plug in her ass. A gag muffles the noises escaping her mouth.

The tree's bark has scratched little red marks down her chest and belly. She takes a deep breath, inhaling the pepper and mint of the pine tree, Jack's musky cologne and sweat, the smell of the lake on the warm spring breeze. Her vision is dark, but in the distance, Charlie hears the faint rumbling of a motorcycle winding its way through the narrow forest path.

"That'll be our last butch of the night." Jack's hand trails up Charlie's spine to the back of her neck, gripping firmly.

"Are you ready to be a good boy for us now, Charlie? Have you learned your lesson for misbehaving?"

Charlie's "mhmm" comes through the gag.

"You don't get any pleasure that you don't beg for, boy. You get permission from your Sir and her friends first, do you understand?"

Charlie nods eagerly under Jack's grip. She hears the last bike come to a stop and turn off. Her wet cunt throbs in the humiliation of meeting a stranger like this; all tied up, blindfolded, plugged and gagged and cockwarming a thick dildo. The tongues haven't stopped around her clit or her ass and her legs are shaking.

The only thing holding her up is the tree, the nylon rope encircling her wrists, and the two pairs of hands gripping her hips and thighs. Her throat trades whimpers for moans and she's starting to get close when –

"Stop," Jack orders the two butches on their knees.

Charlie swallows the pitiful whine that threatens to escape her mouth. She trembles and slumps against the tree, but Jack keeps a steady grip on her neck, holding her up.

"What's a matter, boytoy? You wanted to cum or something?" she mocks.

"Too fuckin' bad, prettyboy. We all get to use your slutty holes tonight before you even get to think about cumming on my dyke dick."

At this, Charlie can't help but groan. Her cunt throbs, thinking of Jack inside her.

"Now, I think you've had enough of your punishment, so I'm taking these toys out of you. When I untie you, you're gonna be a good boy and not touch yourself while you wait for our cocks. Got it?"

"Mhmm."

Jack unbuckles her gag and pulls it out of her mouth, smearing her spit around her lips and fingerfucking her mouth, growling when Charlie sucks on her fingertips.

"Fucking slut," Jack mutters. Charlie's too dumbstruck to whisper, "Thank you, Sir," but she thinks it – *thank you for making this dream come true, thank you for this pleasure, this denial, this teasing, this ache.*

Jack brings her hand down to the dildo, fucking Charlie a little with it before dragging it out of her body.

"Christ, you're so wet," she curses. Charlie squeaks in agreement. Jack twists the small metal plug, slowly pulling it out of her ass. She exhales in quick pants – "Oh, oh, oh" – as Jack pulls it out and hands it off.

Jack's body heat leaves her backside and Charlie feels the rope loosening from her wrists. The rope falls to the ground, the blindfold lifts from her face, and Charlie turns and locks eyes with the new butch who's just joined them. An oddly familiar butch with a mullet and tattoos. Oddly familiar, like from the New Year's Eve kink party. Eli.

Oh my God, Charlie thinks. She flashes back to the night of the kink party, Eli's compliment on her scene with her friends, the offer to play downstairs, the way she was standing in front of them naked in her cuffs, collar, and boots, still trembling from her orgasms.

Now, again in nothing but her boots, legs shaky like a fawn's, she realizes that she's never met Eli while wearing clothes.

The shock on Eli's face quickly fades to a smirk. Looking smug, their eyes travel up and down her body with a hungry gaze.

"Charlie... Fancy seeing you here. We have to stop meeting like this. I mean, or not. I'm happy to keep meeting you like this..." Eli's sentence trails off as their gaze travels back down Charlie's naked body, dark curls between her legs, brown nipples hard and at attention, blush under her freckles.

"You two know each other?" Jack asks.

"We, uh, met at... Thirst."

"Charlie..." Jack purrs. "A kink party? You're such a slut."

"Yeah, she is," Eli agrees.

She gulps, face hot, feeling lightheaded as she stares at Eli.

"Well, Charlie? Do you agree? Are you a slut?"

Charlie glances at Jack. "...Y-yes, Sir."

A wicked smile grows across Jack's face. "Then prove it," she says. "Get on your knees and take it." She points to the picnic blanket on the dirt.

Jack's black strap hangs out of her pants from earlier, hard and ready for her.

Charlie drools a little and gulps. Her heart thuds in her chest and her vision grows glassy with lust.

"Yes, Sir." She turns to the blanket and brushes past Eli, who smells like tobacco and leather and cologne. She gets to her hands and knees, feeling hot, glancing up at Eli before casting her eyes down in submission. They smirk down at Charlie, taking a step forward.

"May I?" they ask Jack, deferring to her as the Sir of the scene. It makes Charlie so hot the way that Eli asks Jack for permission, like she's owned, like she's an object.

Jack nods. Eli lifts Charlie's chin, examining her face, blush on her cheeks, her gaze toward the ground.

"Look at me," Eli orders.

Charlie's gaze flicks up to theirs, her eyes on fire with need, dark with arousal.

"Good *boy*," Eli praises in a patronizing tone. "So *pretty* for us. What do you need, baby? You need your holes filled?"

Charlie nods.

"Say it."

"Yes! Fuck. I need it."

"*What* do you need, Charlie?"

"I *need* to be fucked, Eli... I need my holes filled with butch cock. *Please...*"

Eli lets go of her chin. "Good boy," they growl. Charlie is hypnotized as Eli unbuckles their black leather belt, unbuttons their Levis, and unzips their fly.

She feels her mouth hanging open, drool gathering on her tongue as she watches Eli withdraw their hard packer and hold it in their hand with a firm grip. Jack does the same, walking around them to stand behind Charlie.

On her hands and knees, on a blanket on the ground in the middle of the woods, Charlie realizes that it's dusk now, growing darker. Just as Jack and Eli settle in to fuck Charlie, the remaining butches flick on their motorcycle headlights, creating a spotlight on Charlie as she blushes and opens her mouth wider for Eli's strap.

"So eager to get filled, aren't you, boytoy?" Jack asks from behind, her calloused fingers dipping into Charlie's wetness and tracing it around her clit. Thighs trembling, Charlie fights to keep her arms stable and her gaze on Eli steady.

"Yes, Sir," she answers obediently. "Yes I am. So eager – please. That feels good, Sir, fuck, I – *oh.*"

The *oh* slips out when Jack's tip meets the opening of her wet, swollen cunt. Eli's strap slides against her tongue, and both of them rub against her wet openings as Charlie loses words and can only repeat, *"Ohhh."*

The two butches each slide inside her holes at the same time, filling Charlie up and drawing a progressively louder moan of pleasure from her throat as Eli's strap muffles it in equal measure.

Jack's three other friends shift to watch Charlie. She sees them in her peripheral vision before her eyes flutter closed, mouth wide open for Eli, legs spread for Jack. Charlie lets little noises escape her with the sensation of being full and fucked. Eli grabs her short black hair, forcing her eyes back up to them.

"Louder, boytoy," they order her. "You were so loud for me in front of the crowd at the kink party. Don't hold back now that my cock's in your mouth."

Jack's hand is warm and calloused on the back of her neck, pushing her deeper onto Eli.

"Go on, boy. Show my friends your appreciation for making your little boywhore dreams come true."

"Ohhhh," she groans as Eli sinks deeper into her eager throat.

A voice from the crowd chimes in, "You like being slutted out by a bunch of butches, huh, boytoy?"

She responds with a strangled, affirmative noise.

Jack fucks her slowly and deliberately. Jack's in no hurry, happy to tease and torture Charlie's cunt for as long as she can take it. Eventually, the butches begin to take turns with her mouth, but Jack remains buried inside her, thrusting at new angles and paces and pressures to find out what sounds she'll make in response.

The sensation of being filled, overwhelmed, used by a group of strangers – dykes – butches – lets her give in, submit to pleasure, release her fears, let go, set herself free. It feels like pleasure, spark, ache, relief, bliss.

When she's sucked every butch's cock in the woods outside of Beaverton, Ontario – at least, she's pretty sure – when Daddy with the snake tattoo has their strap in her mouth and when Jack's fingers are on her clit, stroking softly, and she's close… she finally, finally dares to pull the dildo out of her mouth and ask (beg):

"Please, Sir, please, Daddy, can I cum? Please?"

"How 'bout it, Jack?" Daddy snarls, fucking themselves back into Charlie's mouth an inch deeper.

"Don't you fucking dare," Jack orders Charlie in a stern voice that only makes her pussy clench harder.

Noises of protest are muffled by Daddy in her mouth.

"What's a matter, boytoy? Got something to say to your Sir?" Daddy teases, gripping her hair and pulling her off their strap.

"Please, Sir!" she gasps. "Please. I need it. I'm so close and y-you're so hot and – you feel so good inside me and I – need it, Sirrr… I need it…"

"Aww, you need it? Poor thing. How badly do you need it, you pathetic little cumslut?"

"Anything –" Charlie pants. "Anything. I'll do anything. Please."

"Christ, *anything*, boytoy? Don't fucking tempt me…" Jack says as a warning, a threat. "Please, Sir! Anything you want. I just need to cum – I want to cum on your butch cock, Sir. *Please.*"

"Here's the deal, if you want to cum," she says.

* * *

Jack and her friends treat Charlie to many orgasms, so many that she loses count, mumbling "*thankyouthankyouthankyou*" until she's too tongue-tied to talk anymore. When she gasps, "Oh – too much," Jack swiftly scoops Charlie up, waving her friends away, telling them to ride safe.

Jack carries Charlie to a soft pile of blankets and a sleeping bag in the tent she prepared, tending to the small scratches on her torso with alcohol wipes and antibiotic ointment. She cuddles Charlie and showers her with praise and compliments.

Later, in the middle of the night, when it's dark and a little chilly and the only thing keeping a naked Charlie warm is the adrenaline of speed and the arousal of exhibitionism, Charlie makes good on her deal with Jack.

They fly down the highway on Jack's motorcycle while Charlie is wearing nothing but her shiny black boots and Jack's helmet. She's never felt more free.

The vibrations of the rumbling bike, combined with the toy tucked between Charlie's legs, have her bare thighs shaking.

It's not long before Charlie's orgasm sparks and ignites like a hot motorcycle engine, pleasure and heat engulfing her body, and she cums again with her borrowed motorcycle helmet muffling her cry.

19

Salt by Macsen K. Rhaff

Eucalypts

Sweat darkens the hair on her legs. Short black strands sticking to her skin. Trails of perspiration run like creeks through the dirt on her calves and drip into the wool of Hard Yakka socks.

Her boots are crusted with mud. A dusty coating settled into leather over time with the fresh dark layer of today. I watch the way she places her feet. Each step agile, yet heavy. There's a firmness to the way boot meets ground, like she knows exactly where she belongs.

She walks in front of me on the trail. We'd fallen easily into this formation as the path narrowed. She in front, me behind.

Above, the eucalypt leaves catch a glimpse of afternoon sun, the clouds shifting to let light seep into the forest. The twisted grey trunks burn momentarily sunset orange. She stops mid-step, my boot landing just behind hers. We're so close we're almost touching. She turns, face alight with the sun, eyes bright with awe. That tough butch demeanour cracked open a little to reveal an unreserved smile. She looks handsome like this. And I could almost reach out to touch her face where the golden light softens her skin. But I know better than to be so bold.

Her gaze shifts, from the trees to me. There's an ease to her confidence, in the way she fixes her eyes to mine. I want to look away, but feel strangely compelled to hold her stare. Stifling my own breath, as though the rise and fall of my chest might reveal too much. She watches me like she's looking for something. When the burden of scrutiny becomes too much, I let my eyes drop shyly to the ground. I catch her slight smile in my peripheral vision as she turns around, saying nothing, and continues down the trail.

Nettle

The path grows gnarly, clustered with tree roots and rocks. A steep decline towards the sea. Time slows with each careful step. Our knees taking the strain of our descent.

She grunts a little with the effort and the sound stirs something in me.

I smell salt and the slight stench of seaweed. Clouds take back the sky and a mist settles amongst the trees. Shadows deepening beneath the canopy. Goosebumps prickle my skin. The leaves above us mimic the sound of the waves crashing below.

Suddenly, I'm losing my balance, rushing towards rock and mud and leaf litter. My hands outstretched to catch my fall. A sharp sting. Hands deep in nettle. I hold my breath a moment, feel the prickling heat of it in my skin. Like fire.

She reaches out a hand to help me up. Something in me wants to say no, wants the dignity of my own strength. But I know better than to bruise her pride. So I let her guide me to my feet. Her hand rough and sturdy. Calloused fingertips against my skin. Like fire.

"You ok?" She asks.

"I can handle it" I say, the tingle of pain tugging at me, the part of me that knows my own strength. Knows how much I can take. She sees it. I can tell by the way she glances at me. Her eyes daring me to prove the truth of it. Her hand clenching slightly, a muscle memory, fingers ready for a fist-full of hair, my head pulled back, my breath reduced to gasp.

"I know you can" she says. Her eyes shifting to my calf, tracing the line of blood that drips from my grazed knee. "I know."

Rocks

When the trees open to the sea, we are met with the torrential crash of waves beating against rocks. The sky shifting greys, bleak and unforgiving. Looming cliffs fading into the mist behind us.

"Take your boots off" she says without looking at me. Her hair is alive, a frenzy in the wind. I do as she asks, leaving my shoes and socks at the edge of the tree line. She keeps hers on.

Though we are no longer on a trail, we stay in formation, her in front, me behind.

There is no soft sand, only the sharpness of broken shells and the jagged edges of a million shifting stones. She strides forward, boots crunching against rocks. My feet are tentative and slow. Each step a sacrifice. She turns to look at me and I see it then, the fierceness in her eyes.

She says nothing, just lets the sound of the heaving ocean wash over us, as she watches each step I take. I know better than to wince. I have too much to prove. I let the soles of my feet be the price to be paid.

When I am close to her, she turns and keeps walking. I keep pace.

I am not like the other boys she knows. Who walk in sunlit parks and lean soft and gentle into her arms. I am something else entirely. I crave the kind of beauty only found here, in the unrelenting harshness of this landscape. She sees it in me. And I know how much she needs it. How she has longed for a boy strong enough to withstand the violence that yearns to pour out of her.

Blood

"I love this place" she says, eyes fixed on the ocean. "It feels like it could tear you apart, if it wanted to." Something in her tone catches inside my guts. I'm hardly taking a breath now, like I'm waiting for something.

Her fingers are cold when they reach for me. An unexpected tenderness as they trace the shape of my face. "You're a sweet boy, aren't you?" she says, her hand running down the length of my neck. Soft at first. Then slowly the sharp edges of her nails, pressing deeper and deeper. I watch her face change. The shifting beauty of her, like the forest, like the sea. This land can sustain you and it can take your life. She is like that. And I want nothing more than to be at her mercy.

"Take off your clothes." She says, calm like she knows I will obey. I unbutton my flannel shirt as she watches. Pull my singlet over my head, my nipples met with the pinch of cold air. The warmth of the day has disappeared with the sinking sun and the sea carries its chilled breath into my skin.

She nods her head ever so slightly, a gesture to say keep going. I unbuckle my belt, pull down pants and jocks. My clothes, a rumpled pile on the rocky beach. Quietly she observes, as I stand vulnerable and exposed, fearing the softness of my skin too tender against the backdrop of this fierce place. But in her eyes I see the greediness of lust. And I sense my own power then, in the way my body brings out something untethered in her.

She takes my breast in her hand. "You know how to do as you're told, don't you?" I let her pinch my nipple beyond the point of pleasure. She doesn't let go. I don't move. I need her to know she's right, I can be the boy she needs. I take deep breaths, let them out slow, until she releases and the pain is over.

The wind picks up. Whips sea spray into my exposed skin. Waves crash into each other with unrelenting fury. I feel the way she changes too, eyes narrow, stern. Her hand around my throat. I can't breathe.

When she pushes me to the ground there is no resistance. I am strong, but I know better than to fight against the tide. I let out a gasp as my knees hit rocks. See the way she smiles as my face contorts.

Her muddy hiking boot pushes against my chest, forcing me backwards.

I knew she would take whatever she wanted. How she needed this, a chance to be untamed. How I am the boy for it. The one who needs this too. Her hands, claiming me. The grip of her fist on my throat. The weight of her knee on my chest. The slap of her palm on my cheek.

When she forces my legs apart I'm already dripping wet, my dick swollen and hard. She knows before her fingers reach it, sticky themselves with me.

She shoves her soiled fingers into my mouth so I can taste the sweet bitterness of myself. To remind me that I want this.

Her hand is rough on my dick. The kind of roughness that tells me this is not for my pleasure. She rubs my cock until it's so sore I almost beg her to stop. But when she pulls away I'm desperate with longing. She knows from the look in my eyes how much I need it. She does not give it to me. Instead she watches me squirm. The smile on her lips both callous and cheeky.

"You're a good boy" she says, breaking the silence, and my body lets go, softens itself into the rocky shore. Settles.

I lie there unmoving and watch her unbuckle her belt, unzip her fly and pull out her cock. She forces her hand down against my chest and pushes herself inside me. "Sssh" she says to quieten me when I cry out. Covering my mouth with her hand. Pushing deeper. All of my body wants to gasp, but I can barely breathe.

"Take it" she growls. Her voice unrestrained.

A change has come over her, like the fury of the ocean that knows no limits. There is nothing left now but the thrust of her own cock. The rawness of her need.

With each plunge of her hips the flesh of my back scraps against sharp rocks. She thrusts deeper. Back and forth. Jagged edges tearing at skin. The searing heat of pain. Back and forth. Scratches deepening into cuts. Back and forth. Trickles of blood warm against my skin.

She does not stop. She will not. She cannot.

Tears run down the side of my face. "You can take it" she says firmly. Knowing that I can.

She fucks me until I cannot feel my body anymore. Only the burning flame of pain. Only the light headedness of surrender. In that moment, I cease to exist. I become this place. I become the rocks stained with my blood. I become the ocean reaching towards us. I become the wind enclosing us.

Her growls sound far away, the grunt of her, the final screams she lets out. She howls as she comes and I return to my body then, feeling the release of her.

Salt

We enter the water like a sacrifice. The sea is hungry. Licking blood from my wounds.

This is no passive ocean, it will take what it wants. She understands. Knows what it means to take what you need. Yet I see the way even she is humbled here. By the force of something greater than her.

I sense the sea's desire. To devour me. As it drags me down. I feel her hand gripping me. Beneath the surface we struggle for breath and light and rebirth. She does not let go. Until the sea releases us. Casts our bodies onto the rocks, amid salty froth and the rush of water tumbling stones back into the ocean.

My chest heaves with the relief of air in my lungs. Salt water dripping down my throat. I feel her calming her own breath. Long deep inhales. Everything slows. The landscape shifts around us. A settling of the wind, a quietening of the trees as they soften into stillness. I let myself soften too. The edge of the sea shifting back and forth over us. Like the rise and fall of her chest. As she holds me. Arms like anchors. My bloodied flesh stinging with the sea's offering. Of salt and redemption.

20

A Lover's Guide to Warning Bells by Des DeVivo

It's been a hard year for us.

I've taken him here to see how the surgery has changed things; not just within his body, but between ours.

I hope the ocean will remedy what the surgery has not.

Or has yet to.

I'm trying to be patient. They've said it'll just take time …

But 'they' promised a lot of things that haven't been true about this experience .

Ignoring those desolate feelings and leaving them behind in the backseat of the Jeep, I heft our cooler down to the sand. Wiping sweat from my brow, I notice my boi adjusting his aviators, looking longingly towards the sea.

My thumbs hook onto the denim belt loops around his muffined waist, and his breath hitches as I reel him into me.

He doesn't relax, but I don't let go.

Is this a boundary? I don't know.

We've never really discussed them. We've never needed to.

Instead of plotting emergency protocols, I simply listen for the quiet warning bells. There's no escape plan for him, just an abort-mission on my part. If there's a tingle in the air, a shift of molecules against the hairs on my arms, I know, then, to stop.

One's going off, now – I see it in the way his pulse flutters in his neck as he cranes his face away from mine. Those bells have been tolling a lot lately; in his airwaves, in my heart.

So I let him go.

He glances back at me, almost apologetic, before striding off towards the sea. I lay out our blanket and fall back onto my hip, watching in wonder as he becomes doll-sized, though mentally strays no further than he's already drifted.

It's not his fault, the distance.

I can't imagine what it must feel like to be carved out, then expected to just 'be better' on the other side. Surgery doesn't remedy fear, but no one tells you that.

No one warns you about the lingering side effects hidden amongst gift wrapped relief.

He's been struggling with it – the Mederma, the Bio-Oil, the bathroom mirror.

Yet here, in the bright open air of the coastal sidelines, I watch him revert to who he was before the knife.

He's like a nebula, with the energy of star particles swirling around him.

An indomitable force of nature that doesn't know his own power.

Doesn't know he *is* his own power.

I swear, sitting here on the shore, I can see the waves receding, not because of the missing moon's distant pull, but because of the gravity of him. They tumble up against his knees, soaking his jorts, as if he's called the waves to come sprinting into his arms like a familiar pet.

The way he used to jump into me ...

His laughter challenges that of the sea and carries on the wind that smells of salt and my boi's sweet perfume. I breathe in, close my eyes, and memorize the nectarine taste of this moment.

I let him play as long as he likes, because he deserves this; and it's my reward, too.

A shadow casts and the blanket shifts as his weight slots in beside me. I crack one eye open, tracing the outline of his torso, armored by a thinning tank, wondering what happened to the daring boi who was riding shotgun, sparkling with the determination of the PCH's wind tousling his curls.

"Did you want to take your shirt off?" I ask.

No – I read the answer, swift and clear, in his body language. Then in his eyes. But he averts his gaze and picks at a string on the blanket instead of answering verbally.

It's not my right to push, but it's my responsibility to.

That's the definition of our partnership, after all.

But then ...

Something changes.

The same molecules which I've grown to read like braille shift into something legible. And agreeable. But I don't know if it's his courage fortifying or his vehemence crumbling under the pressure of my expectantly cocked eyebrow.

"Um ... Sure."

I tilt my head as he continues to avoid me.

"You don't have to." I give him the out, reminding him only of the oath he'd made to himself. The whole reason we are here – because he'd said he was ready.

His eyes scan the shoreline, cautious of the public's keenness to gawk. I follow his gaze, and simultaneously we pinpoint shapes that linger in the distance. Too far to be active onlookers, but close enough to pop the bubble of isolation that his vulnerability often requires.

However, we are only ever as alone as we allow ourselves to be. Privacy is a myth that we can choose to perpetuate or not.

I know what's under his shirt. I saw the worst of it. But now that it's healed, he hides it only after the lack of my necessity has given him agency ... and shame.

"N–No," he says, eyes still trained on the faraway figures. "It's ok. I want this."

And that part is true. Or at least it was, before we left the house.

Coy fingers snag at the hem of his tank top and he pulls it up.

Bravery does not have to be loud.

It can be quiet.

Quiet as the sound of a shirt slipping over one's head.

There. He shimmies, flushed like cotton candy. Uncomfortable. Cute.

And I see that who he is today isn't so different from who he was before. His gentle essence, despite all of life's obstacles, remains. I wonder at his ability not to be hardened by unfortunate circumstances, while I worry that I've pickled in resentment and become bitter. So I make the conscious effort to slow and be gentle; not necessarily because it's what he wants, but because it's what I need.

My boi exhales the stale breath he's been holding as the tank slips from between his fingers and his scar meets direct sunlight for the first time.

Sometimes it's plum, sometimes it's peach. Today it's glistening with sweat. I want to put my mouth on it, but I know his defenses will shock me like an electric fence if I get my tongue too close to flesh that hasn't yet learned how to be touched without tingling with a painful numbness the doctors call normal, but isn't.

He scoots closer. Heat and hunger mount within me.

He looks delectable; head tipped back, chest exposed, alabaster belly blinding.

… all mine.

He's mine.

And he shines with the growing knowledge that he belongs to himself now, too.

"Lay back," I say.

"Why?" he whispers, on guard against a world that's only ever hurt him. And while I occupy that world, I'm not the source – just the man who survives the brunt of his wildfires until they've exhausted themselves into harmless embers of regretful smoke.

He does as I say without further contest, easing back onto the blanket.

"Close your eyes."

This he does, too.

Although his movements are timid, the breath escaping his lips is a needy hush that I know well. I slick my tongue between the pads of my thumb and index finger, dampening the digits that drag through sand, collecting pebbles as if they're magnetized.

Perhaps they are ... to me, to us, to our revitalization.

My hand ghosts over the softness of his navel, his stomach, the boldness of his bare chest. My fingertips, coated in the coast, find the perfect pink of his nearest nipple.

He sighs like the sea; humid, wild, saltine.

I haven't touched him like this in so long.

The grit of the sand becomes my teeth, leaving my eyes free to watch as his own flutter with an ecstasy he hasn't allowed himself since that first doctor's appointment.

Let me, let you; I chant with the pinch of my fingertips that roll counter, then clockwise, then back again. I close my eyes and listen to the methodical swell and subsequent crash of the waves on the sand and let that be my metronome. Usually I keep to the frequency of his heart, which ramps steadily as he nears release, but this moment isn't about completion.

Just connection.

If only everyday could be like this, I think, and daydream about all the ways this cloying moment could develop – even as I scold myself for making wishes of the future instead of steeping in the present. This moment, for months, was all I ever wanted.

And here we are.

Yet, here I am. Already living in the past.

I open my eyes and take in his blushing brilliance, reminding myself of the vows I made, in contrast to the ones he's made to himself.

Take care of this boi, I promised.

And, fuck, would I ever. If only he'd let me.

The way, I realize, he's letting me now ...

Scar tissue and the cosmos have long been forgotten; he's plagued only by my fingerprints and the fever in his cheeks. His hands are bound by fistfuls of our shared blanket, and his knees butterfly wide.

A consent that nature never seeks.

Unlike the ocean, which pillages anything in its path, I ask permission.

And I am granted it.

Because although my boi knows that I would make love to him anywhere, despite the oppressive shadows of lingering strangers, he also knows I would never break the trust that he extends.

So I do as I have always done, and love him best by listening.

I listen for bells as I lean down to rap at his lips for entry.

He opens.

I listen for bells as my tongue dances around the maypole of his.

He moans.

I listen for bells as the sureness of his grip guides my sandy hands South.

He shudders.

And I smile; with the knowledge that I'm listening for bells that have ceased to toll.

21

Sunk by The IE

You are outside of me.
 I am inside of me.
 There are two fine barriers of skin between us.
 One containing the ocean of me and the other containing the ocean of you.

If I let you touch my skin, will the ripples start? Will they build until they are waves? And if the waves begin, will *It* awaken; that monster inside? If the monster does rouse I will have to pretend that it has not, so no one outside of me knows of the beast that I carry in my internal sea.

First, I think you could not possibly cause ripples for you are a stranger and I am in love with another. All I want is sex. You are here to give that to me. So how about I allow the creature to stir just a little? I tell myself I can do this. It is my monster and I can control it.

And so I let you stroke me, and soothe me, and at first, I feel only tiny ripples- none that could reach where the monster sleeps... but my ocean leaks out a little, through my eyes. You are not the person I love, and it hurts that you are not them. I have so much hurt. The tears disappear into the pillow.

Back to the action. Of having sex.

Sex will help me forget.

You tie me up.

You blind fold me.

This is good, my tears will not be seen.

I succumb to you.

I need this.

This act of forgetting.

You start your work, your deft hands make their way inside and I gorge on your fingers as my cock swells hard and new moisture leaks out between my thighs, from the soft warm lagoon of my cunt. But this is not my ocean- I tell myself- it is a different pool, surely? An estuary, I tell myself; a loch, a lake, a mere that refills and spills.

This act of forgetting is also dependent on what I tell myself.... .

I repeat that my ocean is sealed safe inside. You, a stranger, cannot possibly know how to stir my inner sea.

Your hands, so capable, relax me further. I slide onto you and suck you into me. I check my thoughts and yes, my lies of control are holding strong.

I feel the monster stir but I keep it sleepy. Lull it. Hush it down again.

It slides its soft somnambulant tentacles against themselves, it slithers, it slathers and slowly unfolds dreamily within me. Its feelers slide down the raw inside of my flesh, following the inside of my thighs- where the skin is thin and I wonder how skin so thin can contain so much feeling inside. But it holds, this dam of flesh, and you have no idea, from your vantage point outside, that a monster is moving so deeply. You have no idea what you are messing with... and I'm not about to tell you.

"Keep low monster," I command "Don't think to extend your pleasurable limbs up any higher!"

But through my belly it now crawls, heaving its heated form up through me as more sensual tentacles uncurl and curl through my ocean. My bound arms are taken control of, and they pull against their bonds.

Like a glove now, I am being worn by this beast. I am too far gone in my grindings against you to keep my defences high as the last of its curious probes caresses its way toward my chest. It has found the secret rein between my cunt and my heart and it unrolls itself through me to bridle its quarry; my bloody red pump.

The tension between my heart and my cunt pulls taut like a strap made of intangible fibres. No monocle, no spectacles, no magnifying glass, no electron microscope, no X-ray, no scanner with injected contrast dye, no post mortem or dissection with the finest diamond-bladed scalpel will ever find this secret tether.

This strained cable can only be felt, as all sensations are felt, through the hot red liquid inside me. I quiver, break and submit.

I am fresh emotions.
   The loch of my control levers open.
   I start to flood.
   Currents of needle thin strikes puncture my insides. Muted rhythmic tides pulse through me.
   A swell builds.

Waves make ruin of my senses and I submit in passive eclipse... call it lust, call it love, call it frustration, call it foolishness. For that is what it surely is, this folly I feel for you, and you could risk to feel for me, in this moment of my surrender.

The monster has its soft, warm arms full of me now.

Want.

I want you, Sir.

I want more of you and more of you until your ocean is in me and I can spill across and swim into you.

I want to dissolve in you, Sir.

I want to become meaningless in you.

And so, you, stranger, you have made your way through my defences. By sliding those precise fingers of yours inside, and fucking my monster awake.

I am yours entirely now, Sir.

You conduct currents and feelings inside me as you orchestrate my pleasure. But you must not touch my heart. For then, I wager, you will find me in my dreams. If you find me in my dreams you will reach me when I am completely open, and there you would run riot along the leash between my cunt and heart. Not that this is what you want... you are lost in your professional duties. You have no idea of the emotional whitecaps that splash up inside me whenever anyone fucks me so well.

"Go gentle, Sir!" I hear myself thinking, but not saying...

"You will stop this now!"

Words I should utter into the air but they stay in my mind...

Instead, I hear myself whimpering for more of you. I want you harder, and I want you deeper, and my cock is engorged, and my ocean is spilling like water from a too-full glass, onto your face and your hands as I stuff myself with you.... And you fill me with your hands.

And I hear my groans as if they are not mine....

And I thrust myself up to you...

And I should have known better than to think I was ever in control at all...

The truth is that I have no self-control. I have led myself to this point with lies.

I know the monster will always awaken when I fuck.

I know I don't care about my heart when my cunt is so hungry.

And I know of the danger lurking in the depths but choose to pretend that this time will be different. It never is.

Even when my heart knows the monster is awake, I do not change tact to save it.

If my heart were a tall masted ship, that presides on this ocean inside, and prefers a still sea to waves. Once the monster is churning the seas around it, I just keep fucking.

I do not fire cannons or set barrels on fire, for the hope that the beast of my lust will relent and leave the hulk of me to survive afloat on life's waters. Life is dull without a monster wrapping its long, suctioned limbs around the masted ship of my soul.

Instead I let my heart, this vessel that normally sails rough seas so well, lie stupidly in a windless moment, as longing takes hold and the tiny sailors in charge of my senses awaken in fright.

Rather than fight, or sail or steer, or do anything resembling self-preservation, they launch themselves like lost, mindless, fear-struck, wooden-headed buffoons, into the water. They leave this most precious thing that beats within me, without a single hope of defence.

Again my ship is claimed by the limbs of craving and the entire hull is enveloped by thick, powerful, slimy arms, and I am claimed by obsession and lust for you, Sir, a person of the purest blue-eyed filth. My mind is dragged to the depths of my desire - to lay amongst the other shipwrecks of all my loves/lusts past... and I have let it all happen again.

"Oh well"... I tell myself... "things could be worse?"

I hear the snapping of timbers inside me.

I let you fuck me raw. You are all suckers now. Your mouth sucks on my mouth, as my cunt sucks on your hand, your lips suck on my cock and you pin me down with your weight and pull me apart with your bulk.

I urge our skin to split between us as I cum. Hard. I weep the ocean from my eyes, mouth and cunt. I weep out my ocean as you demand.
And before I fall.
Into sleep.
You unbind.
My limp arms.

In parting, you take my hand and slide my fingers through the wet cleft of your cunt, and touch your hard cock against the tips of my fingers.
You turn to leave.
Our sea walls automatically resurrect and we are separate once more.
Safe.
From.
It.

The waves die down. The kraken retreats. The tether dissolves.
My heart is left aimlessly sunk in still brine– like a toy ship in bathwater.

I am sunk inside of myself so completely.
And you are simply gone. Outside.

22

About the Contributors

Anna Sansom (she/her) is queer in all regards, kinky, and endlessly curious about how we experience and express our unique sexual selves.

She started writing erotica over two decades ago and has had a full-length erotic novel published and several short stories in anthologies and online. She also used to write the Sex/Life pages for *DIVA Magazine*, and has trained and worked as a sexual surrogate partner.

Her more-than-a-memoir, *Desire Lines*, invites us to ask the questions – and explore the answers – which lead to greater understanding and enjoyment of our sexual selves.

She loves drinking tea, swimming in the sea, and talking to her cats.

Find more on Anna at:

IG: @anna_sansom_writer

FB: @AnnaSansomWriter

Website: annasansom.com

Cash Torn is a trans faggot of dyke experience who grew up in Scotland and now has the privilege of living on Gadigal land in so-called Sydney, Australia with his Good Boy, dog, cat and many many plants. He uses writing as an antidote against shame, adores working in collaboration with other queers, freaks and weirdos and prefers to be naked as often as humanly possible.

Follow him on Instagram @cashtorn

Christian Pan is a writer of erotic fiction whose narratives frequently center the lives and experiences of bisexual individuals. He lives in New York City.

He has published 13 books of erotica, including *At the End of the World*, which won the 2023 Star Recommendation for Erotica from All The Filthy Details; and was a Finalist for the 2022 Golden Pigtails Smut Award for Dark/Taboo Erotica. He has published more than 100 short stories in English, Spanish, and French, which appear in various erotica anthologies.

In addition to writing fiction, Christian publishes book reviews for his Dirty Words blog, and is a contributing writer for both *Dish Stanley's Crush Letter* and Dr. Tiffany K.´s *Artistic Edge Magazine*. He hosts the Pulse Session segment for the monthly podcast, *All the Filthy Details*, and has been the A Club Captain for Patreon´s Queer Erotic Content Creators Club since 2022.

For more information on Christian visit:

https://linktr.ee/christianpan

https://www.instagram.com/christianpanerotica/

https://twitter.com/christian_pan_

Cosimo Vazquez is a Mexican writer based in Melbourne who enjoys exploring new ideas around immigration, embracing futures thinking, and tackling life's challenges with a creative and reflective approach.

Des DeVivo is a queer writer of queer stories that transmute pain into beauty. Born and raised in small-town Ohio, they now reside in Los Angeles with their husband and three cats.

Follow Des on Instagram @desdevivo.writes

erin riley is a social worker and writer living on Gadigal land. Erin brings a queer lived experience to their professional work and their writing and is fascinated and energised by the power of stories in both understanding and reimagining ourselves. Erin thrives on routine and loves swimming in the ocean. They were a Penguin Random House fellow in 2021, and have been published in *Kill Your Darlings*, *The Guardian*, *Archer Magazine* and various corners of the internet. Erin's debut memoir, *A Real Piece of Work*, came out in

2023.

Follow them on Instagram @erin_j_riley

Jaymie Wagner is a queer, trans, and polyamorous writer living in Minneapolis with her nesting partner, their cats, and an increasingly alarming collection of tiny giant robots.

In addition to a number of published short stories and the "Sing For Me" series of novels published by JMS Books, Jaymie also writes for Catalyst Game Labs and posts "Fractured Fantasies" micro-stories online where she explores different ideas about gender, power dynamics, and monsterfucking, as one does.

She can be found on Instagram and Bluesky @jaymiedwagner.

Jordan Asher (she/they) is a queer femme writer currently living in Los Angeles. She writes fiction that explores the rhythms of queer identity and relentless emotions. Her writing invites readers to explore the complexities of desire, knowledge, love, and candor. Jordan loves the warm glow of the color yellow and her beloved orange cat, Chunk.

Follow Jordan on Instagram @jordan_asher_writes

Leo Wilder is a nonbinary butch lesbian erotica author creating spaces for butch visibility and pleasure. Their erotic stories explore the butch4butch experience and often feature transgender, nonbinary, and gender non-conforming characters.

They publish at butch4butch.com and post on instagram as @butch4butches

Lilith Young is a queer, autistic writer. Her writing explores the dynamics of religion and mental health in queer life. Her current work can be found in the short story collection *Crowded House*, and *Best Lesbian Erotica, Volume 7*, published by Cleis Press. By creating storylines and characters that cross gender and sexual expression boundaries, she hopes that people will feel seen in a way that they are not in mainstream romance writing.

Follow her on Instagram @lilithyoungwrites

Ma Bo is a French-spoken bilingual bisexual trans bean in their twenties, practicing mindful ero-autoportrait in nature, naturist, horny, hairy, wet slut. Le sub dans subvertir, et la hoe dans homme. Writing in English feels like dressing up in a well-fitted gender.

Macsen K. Rhaff is a genderqueer, switchy pervert and writer of liberating trans smut. Wielding words in both healing and horny ways, Macsen infuses their writing with personal experiences of kink, gender and fucking. They currently live on Dharawal land.

Mx. Nillin Lore is an AuDHD, queer, genderflux, and polyamorous author and blogger out of Saskatoon, Saskatchewan, Canada. Nillin has been featured in a number of erotica anthologies and is the author of *"How Do I Sexy? A Guide for Trans and Nonbinary Queers"* and *"Carry On: Unpacking Your Internalized Transphobic and Queerphobic Baggage"* from Thornapple Press.

Find them on mxnillin.com

NoN BiNarY BiRo is a European writer based in London. They have written extensively for the theatre and BBC Radio 4. Most recently they toured the sell-out show *The Butch Monologues* to New York La Mama, TheatreWorks Melbourne, Seymour Centre Sydney, Liverpool's Everyman, London's Soho Theatre, and three times at the WOW festival at the South Bank.

They have several short stories published including: *For Ezra* (Muswell Press), *XXX*, (Muswell Press), *Super-Well* (Anxiety Empire), *Letter To My Future Lover* published in *F, M and Other* (Knight Errant Press), *Gregory* (Brand Magazine). They co-run hotpencil press with Serge Nicholson publications include: *Letter To My Little Queer Self* (2021), *The Butch Monologues* (2017), *There Is No Word For It* (2011). They adapted their poem, *For Ezra*, into the stop motion film *Grand Dandy* (2024) and were in the documentary *Private View* (2023) revealing Sadie Lee's portrait of them. Libro Levi has a Ph.D from UEA in Creative and Critical Writing where they were awarded the HSC Scholarship. They teach Creative Writing in Birkbeck, Guildhall Drama School, and Imperial College and have taught in 5 UK prisons.

Contact Libro via Knight Hall Agency. MBA Lit.
IG:@LibroLeviBridgeman
X:@LibroLeviBridge

Orlando Silver (he/they) is a trans masc writer living and working on Dharug & Gundungurra lands. Orlando is a playwright, performer and erotica writer.

They are the Director of Incision Press: incisionpress.com

His writing can also be found here: orlandosilver.substack.com

Ryder West (they/them) is probably curled up with a third cup of coffee, swatting their two cats off their iPad while attempting to write more smut. Their work centers around trans bodies and the intimacy of t4t sex and relationships. When not writing, they can be found hanging precariously off a rock wall or in downward dog.

Sharon Penance is a white, disabled, neurospicy, chipped polish fat femme, and gold star good girl who likes to get into as much trouble as she can in the backwoods and riverbeds of the Pacific Northwest. She started writing smut during the early days of the pandemic as it felt freeing and fed her in the very best of ways. She writes with deep reverence of the beauty in brutality and delights in bringing discomforting desire to the page ... she might have a little bit of sadist mixed into all that masochism after all.

Follow Sharon on Instagram @tinyqueerlovestories

Mx. Slate Ruins is a mixed race, neurospicy, Transmasc slut who is kinky, polyamorous, queer, disabled, and a soft and brutal Daddy. Slate uses he/him and they/them pronouns interchangeably. Slate is new to writing for the public consumption world and has a real thirst for telling stories of challenging topics with frank vulnerability. They hope their writing helps others explore their own desires, gender, and sexuality. He wants to shift the social narrative to include kinky trans people and highlight our magical experiences. They often draw from scenes of playful deviance both in lived experiences and audacious fantasies. He is a loving sadistic menace and he would love to be witnessed as such through his work. Slate will draw you in with imagery, filling your senses, and then destroy you with gritty and tender sex scenes.

Follow Slate on Instagram @oh4fxsake

Soft Boss is a queer, trans, disabled, punk pervert, lived experience educator, artist & writer living on Gadigal land. A leatherfag, Dominant, top leaning switch with a deep love for Daddy/boy dynamics amongst other filthy fun. Central to all their creative work is a critical exploration of both individual and collective trauma, survival & power. Driven by a deep fascination with the complexities of human connection, they write to make public and visible that which frequently exists in private intimate realms. In writing filthy stories about queer desire, trans embodiment, power dynamics, kink, BDSM, edgeplay, darker perversions, class, deep emotional connection & transcending shame they seek to challenge oppressive conceptions of human worth, celebrate homo sex, turn people on and keep creating whilst fighting for liberation for all.

Follow Soft Boss on Instagram @softboss

The IE originally hails from the Sydney queer scene and has a long history of campaigning for sex worker's rights. Having a background in performance, the IE has previously written plays for screen, radio and theatre.

Currently The IE enjoys writing poetry and fiction/ Sci-fi... and a little smut.

You can find them on Substack: https://theie.substack.com

Follow them on Insta @writer.the.ie

Tiger Salmon (she/they) is a queer artist and writer from Melbourne. She debuted as a writer and publisher in 1988 when she and her partner Jasper launched Australia's first lesbian sex-positive zine, *Wicked Women*. The zine evolved into a magazine that sparked a revolution in lesbian circles of inner city Sydney and Melbourne with parties and events including the infamous Ms Wicked competition. Tiger now conducts exhibitions and events that celebrate the Wicked community. She is currently writing a memoir that tracks her role as an LGBTQI+ publisher and provocateur during the third wave of women's sexual liberation in the early 1990s when the pursuit of pleasure was a powerful political protest. Current discussions about gender, feminism, identity, and queer representation inform her work.

Read more from Tiger on substack: *The Queer Gaze*
website: www.thequeergaze.com

Also by Incision Press

Find more at: incisionpress.com

I Write The Body

Hot, provocative work by 38 international queer and transgender writers. Be seduced by these beautiful stories of queer love and desire, with a large helping of kinky genderfuckery.

In this volume we are ourselves without apology, completely unfiltered. "I Write the Body" gives us stories about trans desire, body reclamation and healing through kink.

Relent

Chapbook of fierce and raw poetry from Orlando Silver.